WITH Every Beat

Book 1 of the Rescued Series

With Every Beat

Cover re-design by: Staci Hart
Editing: Sandra at One Love Editing
Printed in the United States of America by Amazon™ POD services.

If you want to read my other books, keep up with new releases, or buy signed paperbacks, check out my website—

www.AuthorLyndsayMarie.com

Visit me on Amazon —
https://www.amazon.com/author/lyndsaymarie

ONE

Rowan

There's an unrelenting guilt associated with being involved in, and partly responsible for, playing the hands of God; being someone poor soul's only hope that stands between them and meeting their maker. I learned to hide those feelings over time, but apparently only when it involved someone else's life and not my own.

That was the philosophical shit that went through my mind after three glasses of wine, when what I should have been doing was packing my suitcase for the girls' trip that me and my best friends, Katie and Chloe, were going on in a few days.

"What's on your mind over there?" Katie's voice broke into my buzzed and wandering thoughts.

"Nothing, just thinking about this weekend," I said to her, leaving out the part about my complete lack of enthusiasm for volunteering to take on a half marathon, because despite my hatred for running, I needed to do it one more time before Saturday, just to make sure I could in fact drag my body thirteen miles down a stretch of road without dying in the process.

"Hopefully, it's all good stuff," she said. "Just think, only a couple more days and we'll be surrounded by some ridiculously hot athletic men, and consuming as much of the sugar-filled alcoholic drinks and obscene quantities of trashy food we can possibly handle...*after* the race." She gave me a sideways glance.

I just shrugged. "Me? I don't know what you're talking about."

"Yes, you. And you know exactly what I'm talking about, and it wasn't my reference to ridiculously hot men."

"You think you know me so well, don't you? I've been a perfect little angel," I said, batting my eyelashes in complete innocence. Okay, so that was partly—*er*, mostly—a lie. Fine. It was total bullshit. Besides, Katie was the one who brought over the wine...now and every other time she paid me a visit.

"Keep playing dumb. I'd believe you more if you told me you ate a dozen donuts for dinner before I'd believe you were with a man any time recently."

"What's that supposed to mean? Are you calling me a lesbian?" I knew exactly what she meant. I was quite aware of my lack of interest in any relationship or connection in general with the opposite sex.

"Yeah, that's exactly what I meant. I don't care who or what you do, but until then, we need to squeeze in one more practice run. But honestly, Rowe, after this, I'm hanging up my running shoes. I mean, I love you and all, but running isn't turning out to be my thing." It was as if she read my mind. "And I'm the one who thought it would be a good idea."

True statement. She was the one who thought training for and running a half marathon sounded like a good idea. It started out as a stress reliever, something to get my mind off the shit I was going through. Then she started referring to it as *fun*. Two words I was pretty sure I had never used in the same sentence: marathon and fun. It was more like marathon and done. Six months ago, anything that remotely resembled running was one big hell no for me, but I broke down and agreed to it when she said we'd end up in Vegas for our final run.

"I'll never let you live it down either. This is all on you," I reminded her as I flipped through the scant amount of clothes hanging in my closet, thanks to a Marie Kondo TV show binge and drunken purge.

"I wish we could have talked Chloe into running with us. I would've liked to have had the three of us together at the finish line."

"You and I both know Chloe wouldn't run to anything but a Gucci sale, and those don't exist." I reached into the back of my closet and pulled out the only dress I owned, one that hadn't seen the light of day in over a year and held it up for Kat's approval. "Whatcha think about this one?"

She sat up on my bed and faced me. "Ooh-la-la. Sexy! I like it. Wait. Are you finally, after all this time, going to put yourself out there? Maybe just a little bit?" She scrunched her face and pinched her fingers together.

"Ha!" Put myself out there? Was she serious? "No, Katie, I am not going to put myself out there. I haven't put myself out there in years, and I have zero plans of doing it this weekend. But I am going to be in

Las Vegas with my two favorite girls and I want to feel somewhat normal again."

"Well," she said, "whenever you're ready, let me know."

I didn't even need to see her face to know she was grinning from ear to ear. She'd been trying to convince me to let her set me up with someone for a couple of months.

"You'll be the first to know." My first challenge would be keeping up with those two in the looks department. I hadn't put forth near the effort on myself in a long time as either of them did on a daily basis. Katie spent more time on her makeup alone than I did on my entire morning routine. Her face was always smooth and flawless, and most of the time I couldn't tell where her foundation ended and her bare, porcelain skin began. Her long, straight-as-a-board, platinum-blonde hair never had a single flyaway. And Chloe was a freaking magician with a curling wand. For as long as I'd known her, she kept her shoulder-length dark auburn hair in loose, bouncy curls that could withstand everything from category five hurricane winds to Memphis's 100 percent humidity. Me? Most of the time, my long, dark brown wavy hair was kept twisted in a tight bun or some kind of braid. And my entire wardrobe consisted of practically nothing but leggings and a stretchy T-shirts.

"Well, you're getting away from here. It's a start," she said. "You need to lighten up. Who knows, you might meet the next man of your dreams. They don't call it Sin City for nothing."

"Ha." Clearly that was the wine talking. I basically emanated *fuck-off* vibes. "Thanks for the encouragement, but I'm perfectly fine with things the way they are right now. Let's just get through our trip, and *maybe* when we get home I'll throw myself back into the deep end of the dating pool. Promise. But don't get your hopes up. The only *sin* I want to commit is in the form of a Bavarian cream donut." Because, despite her confidence that I'd eaten a dozen donuts for dinner, those were the one thing I'd entirely given up since I took up running, and I was pretty sure I was going through withdrawals.

She reached over to my nightstand and topped off our glasses with the last of the merlot. "I know it's gonna be a tough weekend for you, but that's why we're getting you away from this place. Rowe, it's been almost a year. You know it's okay to move on. David would want you to. Hell, he probably would have by now." She climbed off the bed, handed me my full glass of wine, then snatched the dress from my hand. "I'm packing the dress. It's sexy and you're gonna wear it." She spun around on her heels, marched away, and stuffed it in my suitcase.

I huffed. That stupid little black dress still had the tags on it, and it'd been hanging in the back of my closet since the day I bought it. It was supposed to be the dress I wore to celebrate my five-year anniversary to David. But that celebration would never happen.

"So...you wanna go to the park and get one last run over with?" Kat asked.

"Now? Are you insane?"

"No, fool. Not now. I'm off Thursday. How about then? That'll give us a solid two days to recover?"

"You had me worried for a minute. I thought you'd completely lost your mind. Thursday's fine. Let's go first thing in the morning and get this shit over with. I'm tired and need a new hobby."

"Fair enough," she said as she exited my closet a second time with an arm full of clothes that she'd mysteriously conjured up. She stuffed them in my suitcase before heading towards the bathroom. "I'll pick you up."

While Katie was gone, I took advantage of my free moment and sat down at the massive antique wood desk that once belonged to my dad. It was the one thing he treasured more than anything, besides my mom and myself, and the only physical thing left of his that I owned.

I opened my laptop, logged into Dr. Holland's patient portal, and, against my better judgement, cancelled all of my appointments for the foreseeable future. For the first time since I'd started therapy after my wreck, I'd requested a cancellation. No rescheduling, no solid plans of going back. It was time to start moving on. I wasn't sure if the relief I felt came from canceling my therapy sessions or possibly from the fourth glass of wine I'd just downed thanks to Kat's refill.

As soon as I shut my laptop, Katie walked up behind me and wiped her wet hands on my face. "Whatcha doing over here? Finally decide to sign yourself up on one of those dating websites?"

"Ugh. You brat. No, I am not resorting to virtual dating, yet. I'm cancelling my appointments with Dr. Holland, if you must know."

"Woah. You sure that's a good idea? I mean, isn't this weekend what you've been building your sessions around? Like, the whole reason you started therapy?" I couldn't see her face, but I imagined it looked something like a stern-faced mother would give her child knowing they were about to make a poor life choice and there was nothing she could do about it.

"I guess. I just want to be able to go on our trip and actually enjoy myself without reopening any wounds right before we leave. Ya know? If I need him, I have his number."

She wrapped her arms around me and hugged my neck. "Okay. You know me and Chloe are going to be with you. I mean, we're no professionals, but we at least know how to get you drunk."

"Tell me about it. And thanks for being here. I'm glad I have y'all. Except for when you act like a damned kid."

"You love it," she said. "Hey, not to change the subject on you, but have you heard from your mom lately? Is she still on her *tour de France*?"

I rolled my eyes. Anita Fudge, aka, my mom. We were never really close, but I loved her just the same. "Yeah, I actually talked to her about a week ago. She and Sam were headed to Switzerland next. She said she'd be off grid for a bit, but they'll be stateside in a couple of weeks for the holidays."

"Wow! Switzerland? That sounds incredible. One day I'm gonna marry me a man who can take me around the world at the drop of a dime." She spun around before falling back on my bed.

I just laughed. Kat definitely had the beauty and personality to find that kind of man. "I have no doubt you will. Maybe you'll meet the man of *your* dreams in Vegas."

"Maybe." She sighed. "One day. And ya know what? I don't even hate her for it. Good for her going out and living her best life."

"Yeah, good for her." Unfortunately, my mom's best life cost my dad his.

♡♡♡

"Not bad for our next-to-last run," Kat said, as we loaded ourselves into her car.

It was early winter in the South, which meant Mother Nature acted like a hormonal teenager. One day she was sweet and brought warmth into your world; then, on that very same day for no reason whatsoever, she'd get pissed off and turn into a frigid bitch, making you question all of your life's choices. Today she was having a good day that was perfect for a jog in the city park.

I tried to hide the fact that I was still out of breath as I buckled my seatbelt. "Yeah, not too shabby. Let's hit up the Dunkin Donuts drive-thru on our way out. I need food."

She cut her eyes at me as we pulled out of the park. "Really, Rowe? You can't be serious."

Oh, I was serious.

Half an hour later she dropped me off at home with my egg white sandwich and black coffee. No donuts. No sugar. Total bummer. As I ate my breakfast and sucked down my coffee like it was my last meal, I sat back and looked around the house that had been my home for the past few years. I'd moved in with David right after we got engaged on our one-year anniversary together. It was where we were supposed to raise a family and spend the rest of our lives together. Even with him gone, the house still felt like *ours*...just different.

I had no idea what was going through his mind when he thought he needed a 2400-square-foot house. Guess he never planned on not being around to enjoy it. The thought to sell it and completely wash my hands of it had crossed my mind a few times, but I wasn't quite ready to let it go.

I shot Chloe a text to see if she wanted to hang out since Kat already promised to help out on her parents' farm.

Me: You wanna come over tonight or are you gonna to be tied up?

I inserted a handcuff emoji just for fun. Her response was almost immediate, so I knew at least her hands were free.

Chloe: Ha ha. Actually, Mia set me up on a date with someone. I can come over after? Shouldn't be too late.

Me: Have fun, be safe. I'll be waiting.

It was just after nine later that night when I heard a frantic *bang, bang, bang,* on my front door. Katie had a key and Chloe never knocked. She either barged in or repeatedly rang the doorbell until I answered.

I snuck up to the door and another *bang, bang, bang, bang* echoed as I went to stick my eye up to the peephole. I jumped back, held my breath, then looked out.

It was Chloe, looking mad as hell, still dressed to the hilt in a skin-tight burgundy mini-dress and a pair of four-inch sparkly gold heels.

I unlocked and opened the door. "What a surpri—"

She threw her hand up and cut me off mid-sentence as she stormed past me. "Not a word."

"Okaaay."

She clomped back and forth on my hardwood floors with her head down. "You would not believe the night I just had." When she stopped pacing, she looked up at me with tears in her eyes. "I am so fucking mad right now, Rowan, I could spit nails."

"Well, then tell me what the hell is going on, already? How'd your date go, and where in the hell is your jacket? It's like forty degrees outside."

"I forgot it at the restaurant, hanging up at the coat check. I'll get it tomorrow, or never."

I guided her toward the couch. "Chloe, come sit down. You're making me nervous. Talk to me."

"So, I met my date, Tanner. Right? Super nice guy. He definitely has potential. And, beautiful restaurant, by the way. If you've never been to Capital

Grille, you should go. Anyway, we're talking, same old stuff. I'm putting my feelers out there, you know, just in case this goes anywhere tonight beyond dinner." Tears fell from her eyes. I handed her a tissue. "Thank you." She paused to blow her nose. "So, the night is going great, until we're done and heading out the door, and you wouldn't believe who else was there?"

"Okaaay? Who?"

After a long, dramatic pause she finally said, "Derrick."

"Derrick? So? Y'all broke up months ago." Derrick and Chloe dated for a couple of years. One night, while we were all out together celebrating her birthday with a few friends, he pulled the whole *we need to talk* routine, and instead of him proposing, like she thought he was going to do, he dumped her…in front of everyone.

"So? Rowe, he was on a date!"

"Yeah, and so were you."

She blew her nose again. "Not the same. He was with Jensen!"

"Jensen? Stone? My cousin?" *Holy shit.*

"The only Jensen I know. You get it now?"

"Yeah. Trust me, I totally get it."

Fuck. My. Life.

16

TWO
Rowan

We finally stopped spinning.

Life was eerily quiet.

A bright light blinded me through the cracked windshield.

There was so much pressure in my head and chest. The taste of fresh blood in my mouth was nauseating.

I unlatched my seatbelt and dropped, landing with a hard thud.

We were upside down?

David? I looked over at him and he was crumpled in a heap on the interior roof of our car. The car he'd bought because of its top safety ratings. Safety ratings don't mean shit if you refused to wear your seat belt, David!

I carefully climbed out of the broken passenger window on my hands and knees. I had to get out. I had to get him *out. Smoke billowed up into the sky from somewhere under the hood. Broken glass, shards of metal, and pieces of God only knew what were scattered across the road. Another car was off in a wooded ditch, blinding me with it's one functioning headlight.*

Through the ringing in my ears, I could hear emergency sirens wailing in the distance.

The pain in my legs caused my knees to buckle, but I was grateful they still had movement and feeling in them, but who knew what kind of internal injuries I might have had.

None of that mattered.

I fought my way through the pain, holding on to the bumper of our car, stepping across debris as it crunched beneath my bare feet, working my way around to the drivers' side.

I reached through the busted window, grabbed David by his shirt and yanked on him as hard as I could. I pulled and fought with him to move. His body was too heavy.

Out of nowhere, another set of hands appeared and pulled with me. We pulled together and dragged him out of the car, his lifeless body spread out across the pavement.

He wasn't moving or breathing.

I swallowed down the bile that'd crept its way up to the back of my throat, ignoring my body's need to vomit, and started rescue breathing without ever checking for a pulse.

♡♡♡

I woke up on a sweat and tear-soaked pillow.

It was pitch-black outside. I squinted at the clock on the bedside table. Four forty in the morning. *Holy shit.* Katie and Chloe were going be making their appearances soon. I debated on getting up and making a pot of coffee, and getting my day started. Instead, I flipped my pillow to the dry side, pulled the covers over my head, and went back to sleep.

"Rowe." Someone shook me gently. "Rowan." A soft voice called my name in the distance. "Wake your ass up. You're going to make us late." Then a pillow smacked me on the ass, and I flew upright.

"What the hell?" Katie was standing next to my bed, fully dressed, looking like she was ready to take on the world.

"Rowe, it's twenty after eight. You need to get up or I'll be kicking *your* ass for making us late instead of Chloe's." She turned on her heels and stormed out of my bedroom.

Eight twenty? Holy shit. I overslept? I never overslept. Even considering my lack of routine, I was still an early riser.

I flung the covers back, launched myself out of bed, and made a beeline for the bathroom. One good thing about me being low-maintenance was I could get out of bed, shower, and be completely ready to go before Chloe ever made it here. Because I highly doubted she was waiting for me. But I needed confirmation. I did not want to be the reason we missed our flight. "Is Chloe here yet?" I hollered out to Kat.

"What do you think?" she yelled back.

Perfect. I turned on the shower and stepped under the steaming hot water, knowing I still had plenty of time to get ready.

♡♡♡

"Now boarding flight 1211 Memphis, Tennessee to Las Vegas, Nevada, Gate C-11," a man's voice announced overhead. We were nowhere near our gate thanks to the damned Louis Vuitton store. Chloe insisted on taking a look around, Katie did absolutely nothing to stop her, and my attempts to redirect them failed miserably.

"Isn't it fab?" Chloe beamed as she stroked her new purchase hanging off her shoulder.

"It's perfect!" Katie said.

"Yeah, I love it." I mean, it was a nice purse and all, but damn, we'd already run late once today getting to the airport, and now it was time to board the plane. "Y'all, we need to go, or we are going to miss our flight!"

"Okay, Mom, chill out," Chloe sneered.

We sprinted to our terminal just as the same man's voice made the final announcement to board.

We finally got settled into our seats on the plane, and as soon as we were in the air, we all ordered much-needed drinks from the flight attendant. Chloe got a screwdriver; Kat and I went with our go-to merlot.

Chloe took one sip of her drink. "I knew it." When the flight attendant disappeared out of sight, she dug around her carry-on bag and pulled out two tiny bottles of vodka.

"What the? Chloe you didn't." Katie sounded surprised that Chloe had packed her own mini bottles of alcohol.

"Of course, she did. It wouldn't be Chloe if she didn't."

"Don't judge me." She dumped the contents of both mini bottles into her glass of orange juice and took a sip. "Much better. Cheers."

"Cheers," Kat and I echoed.

Out of nowhere, I was jolted awake as the wheels of the plane hit the landing strip.

"Good morning, sunshine," Chloe said with a devilish grin plastered across her face. "I got some great pics of you with your flycatcher wide open."

"Whatever. I'd rather get caught with my flycatcher open than my dick-trap." Her mouth dropped open, then quickly closed it. I stuck my tongue out at her. "Payback's a bitch."

Kat sat wedged between us, laughing. She smacked each of us on the leg. "Okay, you two. Enough. Let's get off this god-forsaken plane and go have some fun. And no kinky fuckery out of you!" She gave Chloe a pointed look. "Especially you."

"Oh, come on!" Chloe whined with pouty lips. "Pleeeease?"

"Those days are long gone," I said. "For one of us anyway."

As soon as the announcer gave the go-ahead to exit the plane, we collected our overhead bags and trekked to the baggage claim area, where we collected our absurd number of suitcases for a three-day trip, while Kat sent for an Uber. As soon as he pulled up to the curb, we packed the trunk of the car to the brim. Chloe brought two suitcases—one for clothes, one just for shoes—plus a separate bag for hair and make-up, and a carry-on with who knew what packed inside of it besides mini bottles of liquor. Kat had slightly less, but not by much, and I brought my purse and one suitcase.

Our driver eventually swept us away from the airport, weaving in and out of traffic down the strip. Vegas was exactly how I remembered it. Well, what little I'd seen of it, anyway. A few years ago, I spent a week at the MGM Grand for a nursing conference. It was the most boring five days anyone could possibly spend in Las Vegas. I was so worn-out from the miles of indoor walking and endless hours of guest speakers; all I did at the end of the day was eat and go straight to bed.

Vegas is all bright flashing lights, endless traffic, and, oh, you know, just your average joe in some flashy, outlandish costume with his ass hanging out of a sequined thong, parading down the sidewalk at noon on a Friday.

Kat had her face glued to the window as we drove down the Strip. "Can you believe some of the shit people wear in public out here?"

Chloe leaned across Kat to catch a glimpse of the man with his ass hanging out. "Good for him, doing his thing. I should totally ask him where he got that outfit."

I smacked my forehead with the palm of my hand. *Ugh.* I had no doubt she would not only ask him where it came from but stand right alongside him in a matching one, shaking what her mama gave *her*.

22

After ten minutes of side-street entertainment, we unloaded all of our crap at the hotel drop-off and said farewell to our driver.

"Holy shit," Chloe blurted out as we stepped into the lobby of the Bellagio. "This place is freaking ah-mazing! It's even better than the pictures y'all sent me."

That was an understatement. The hotel should have been listed as one of the wonders of the world. The lobby floors were marble with intricate veins of gold and black running through them. Hundreds of multicolored hand-blown jellyfish-like glass figures dangled from the ceiling, and massive mahogany columns skirted the perimeter.

Once we finally checked in, we made it to our room, and it was my turn to freak out. "Holy shit, Katie! This is not a hotel room; this is a palace!" The suite had its own foyer just as outlandish as the hotel lobby. The entire suite had an exotic vibe with metallic walls, royal purple and gold accents, plush everything—carpet, curtains, pillows, linens, and expansive floor-to-ceiling windows that stretched from one end to the other. "I know we agreed to splurge on something a little nicer, but I didn't know you were going to book us the royal treatment."

"You said to surprise you. This is it." She waved her arm like she was hosting *The Price is Right*.

Chloe shoved past us, loaded down like a pack mule with her luggage. "I call dibs on the bedroom with the door."

"Fine by me," Kat said. "I can't wait to wake up to the sunrise over the Strip!"

She was not joking since the only other bed was on the other side of the living room wall that formed a makeshift bedroom facing the strip.

Kat breezed past me, dumped her bags on the floor beside the bed, then made her way out onto the balcony that looked like it was just as big as the entire suite.

I followed behind her. "Looks like we're sharing a bed."

"I'm cool with it," she said. "At least it's a king and it's not like it's the first time we've had to share a bed." She leaned against the railing. "We're gonna need more than a few days to really see this city. It's all just too much to see in one weekend."

"Yeah. We'll have to come back sometime when we don't have to run."

"I totally agree."

Chloe finally joined us. "So, what's the game plan for tonight?"

"Already found the minibar, or did those come out of your purse?"

She took a sip of her drink, then handed a tiny bottle to Kat. "Don't be a hater. I learned from the best. You two forget, I was an alcohol virgin before y'all came along."

"Maybe so, but that was the only kind of virgin you were."

She flipped me the bird.

"Speaking of virgin," I said, "what's the latest with your Jensen and Derrick love triangle? Did you get it all worked out?"

"Yeah," Kat added. "What the fuck's up with that? Can she *not* screw around with someone else's man for a change?" Jensen had a notorious track record with men, and we all knew it.

Chloe rolled her eyes. "Screw the cunt. No offense, Rowe. I know y'all are related and all, but damn, I never saw that coming. That was a whole new low, even for her. And she can keep him. I don't want him back after she's been all over it."

"Good for you! You gonna keep seeing Tanner?"

"Of course. But I might try and meet someone here, too. Mama always said the best way to get over a man is to get underneath another one."

Kat and I laughed at her admission that she was going to try to find someone random to hook up with.

"Wow, sooo, anyway, about tonight, I think we should find a karaoke bar. I've already looked and there's a few close by. I figure we should probably hang close to the hotel since they're gonna be closing down the streets soon for the race tomorrow. We won't be getting very far."

"There's a nightclub downstairs. I don't know if they have karaoke, but we can pop in later and see what it looks like," Chloe said, looking at the map on her phone.

We all agreed. Karaoke it is.

After we practically cleaned out the minibar and Chloe's purse, we spent the rest of the afternoon walking the grounds of the Bellagio. Chloe found the indoor pool, because that was where she would be spending most of her time away from us. Kat and I scoped out the restaurants.

"Well, drink up, bitches," Chloe said raising her last tiny bottle. "We got a long night ahead of us."

"Cheers."

♡♡♡

Chloe and Kat were the queens of dressing up and going out. It took each of them at least two hours to get ready from start to finish. Me? Twenty minutes. Thirty, if I included the shower.

"You good?" Kat asked me as she wrapped her arms around me, resting her chin on my shoulder.

"Yup. Just trying to decide what to wear." I stood beside the bed staring into my open suitcase. I knew exactly what she wanted me to wear, but the thought turned my stomach inside out.

She moved in front of me and rummaged through my bag. As soon as I saw the black satin fabric, my heart sank. "Just wear the damned dress." She shoved it at me, then walked off.

Almost three hours later we were finally ready to go.

Chloe was wearing a black leather mini dress with sparkly black rhinestone four-inch hooker heels. Her hair was curled and fluffed to the max and her eyeshadow was as dark as her dress and finished off with glitter eyeliner.

Kat stood almost six-feet tall in her knee-high leather boots that matched Chloe's dress. Her skin-tight emerald-green dress stopped mid-thigh and showed off half a mile of leg. And, of course, her hair was perfectly sleek and hung halfway down her back.

Against my better judgement, I wore the dress. It was long-sleeved but not in the least bit conservative. It had a plunging neckline and a short skirt with a side slit clear up to my hip. Chloe worked her magic on my hair with her curling wand and gave me what she called "beach waves." I didn't think my hair looked anything like this when I went to the beach. Kat did my makeup. Thankfully, she went lighter on my eyes than she did on her own but begged me to wear her red-wine lip stain.

We finally made our way to the main floor. The hotel buzzed with more people than I'd ever seen in one place. It was long past ten at night and everyone looked like they were just getting started.

A yawn escaped me. "What the hell was that?" Chloe asked. "Did you just yawn?"

I gave her a *no shit, Sherlock* look. "Kiss my ass. It's been a long day."

Chloe hooked her arm underneath mine as she led the way into the club she'd found during her search. "Let's wake you up then."

Linked arm in arm, we wound our way through the already crowded bar and found a pub table at the back that gave us a panoramic view of the entire room.

I perched up on one of the high-top chairs and tugged at the hem of my dress.

"You all right over there?" Kat raised an eyebrow as she sat down next to me. Chloe grabbed the seat on my other side, sandwiching me in between them.

"I'm fine. It's just a little chilly in here. That's all."

She narrowed her eyes at me. "I call bullshit, but I'll give you one free pass."

Chloe raised her arm and signaled the waitress over. I started with a glass of wine, Kat switched up on me and got something with rum, and Chloe went straight for a double shot of vodka.

"Glad we ate before we came here. Looks like we're going to need something to absorb all the alcohol."

Chloe slammed back her double shot and dabbed her mouth with a napkin, being extra careful not to smudge her makeup. "You'll live."

"Yeah, I'll live. But have you ever tried running with a hangover? Or running at all?"

"No and never. Y'all missed out on some delicious food, by the way. What a waste."

"Tomorrow night," Kat said, taking a sip of her drink, "it's game on. We're going to find the most calorie-dense, carb-filled food this city has to offer. I'm gonna eat till I puke."

"I don't know about puking, but I already looked up donut shops and there's one right across the street from here. That'll be my first stop. It's open twenty-four hours, so I might just use what strength I have left and walk straight there after the race."

By the time I'd finished off my third glass of wine, we'd already somehow managed to sing two karaoke songs, and Chloe had talked Kat into taking shots with her.

The waitress came back around with three fancy-looking drinks, plus a glass of water for me.

"Just one. I mean it," I said to Chloe. We toasted to our weekend and took our shots. "Okay, I'll admit. That was delicious. What was that?"

Her speech slurred. "That, my friend, is called a buttery nipple. Mia introduced me to them a few weeks ago. It's my new favorite."

"I might get one more," Kat said.

"Not me. I will not feel like shit when I run." That was a fact. Even though our race wasn't until tomorrow night, I didn't want to waste the day in bed. "I'm gonna carefully walk to the bathroom." We'd been sitting for a while, and I knew my first time standing would be a challenge.

"I'm not far behind you," Chloe said.

"Me either," Kat echoed. "You want us to go with you?"

I stood up, steadied myself using Kat's shoulder, and internally cursed at whoever's idea it was that I wear four-inch hooker heels. Mine. It was probably mine. "Not necessary. Y'all stay here and save our seats. I just gotta pee." I refocused my attention on getting from the far corner of the bar to the bathroom on the opposite side of the room and with any luck back again without breaking an ankle or face-planting the floor.

I squeezed between Katie and the wall. Everything went smooth on the way there, or at least it seemed to in my mind. If everyone else around me had had as much to drink as I had, then they hardly even noticed me. I managed to find the ladies' room without walking into the wrong one, which I'd been known to do in the past. The men didn't seem to mind, but the last thing I wanted

29

was to see a wall lined with urinals and drunk men trying to take a piss with their little willies on full display.

After taking care of business, I gave myself a once over in the floor-to-ceiling mirror before stepping out into the dimly lit hallway. If there was one thing this place was good at, it was setting a seriously dark mood. The walls were dark, and everything was washed in red, orange, and blue lighting. Except the dance floor and bar which were covered in multicolored neon lights and lasers.

I smoothed my hands over my dress one last time for safe measure and gave the hem a tug as my eyes adjusted to the darkness. I made my way back down the hall when the heel of my shoe snagged on the carpet and I dove forward, heading straight for the floor. Halfway down, I slammed into something solid.

Someone's arms wrapped tight around my ribs and hoisted me upright as a rush of air escaped my lungs with an *oof*. The movement was so fast it made my head spin. I gripped his solid arms. "Excuse me," I finally choked out. "I am so sorry." Okay, I was definitely not sorry. It'd been exactly 363 days since I felt a man up close. And there I was, in the arms of a man, pressed firmly against his black button-down shirt-covered rock-hard chest.

Oh. My. God.

I looked up to see his face. Between the darkness and his height over mine and considering my alcohol-induced vision impairment, I could only hope he was as gorgeous-looking as my mind had made him out to be because if he looked anything like he felt and smelled, I was screwed. Well, not that any of it mattered in the grand scheme of things. I was only here for the weekend.

The feeling of him pressed up against me stirred something in my core that sent a long-forgotten buzz through my veins. For a split second, I felt alive again.

"Really? Because I'm not sorry at all." His voice was deep and vibrated against my breast.

Oh, holy hell.

His muscles flexed beneath my fingers.

He moved his face dangerously close to mine. I could feel the heat from his breath against my cheek.

I had a strange feeling he was going to kiss me.

My lips parted. If he was going to pass a move, I was going to let him.

"Can y'all move or get a room? You're blocking the bathroom."

Ohmigod. "Oh, shit. Shit. I need to—." I tried to push him away, but his stance held firm.

He whispered in my ear. "You know her?"

I nodded. I knew exactly who it was. "Chloe," I said in volume low enough for only him to hear me. "We're together."

He locked his arm around my waist, picked me up, and spun me around, pinning me to the wall, shielding me from her with his entire body as she passed by.

I had to get away from him, but the cocky bastard was enjoying this little game he was playing. "Um, thank you? But, uh, I really need to get back to my table."

I closed my eyes and inhaled his strong, sweet, masculine scent one last time, trying to burn it to my memory. Okay, so maybe I was enjoying this just a little bit too.

"Be my guest." His words in my ear sent chills down my spine. We broke contact as he released me from his hold. Keeping a hand on my elbow, he stepped to the side, stretching his other arm out so I could pass by. With my arms folded across my chest, I gave him one last glance over my shoulder, catching a glimpse of him with a cocky smirk on his face, as I walked away.

"Where's Chloe," I asked Kat as I climbed up on my barstool.

"She went to the bathroom to check on you. What the hell took you so long?"

"There was a line."

"Must have been some line. Well, you're just in time. I put our names down for another song," she said all puffed with pride. I thought that sounded like a horrible idea. "You okay? You look pale."

"I'm fine. Just getting tired. Are you sure singing again is a good idea?" I mean, I was all for some karaoke, but we probably should have reconsidered. There were four more empty shot glasses on the table than before I went to the bathroom.

Chloe appeared out of nowhere and laughed as she almost fell trying to sit on her chair. "Karaoke is always a good idea!" I reached over and grabbed her before she hit the floor.

Then the DJ announced Katie's name as if right on cue, and I wanted to run for the nearest exit.

We cautiously made our way through the crowd towards the stage. Chloe led the way, holding on to

Katie's hand. I was right behind Kat, holding on to her other hand as they practically dragged me forward. I couldn't help but scan the room for the mystery man. The bar was filled with probably two hundred people, and I couldn't really make heads or tails of who was who because everyone's face was a blur. But he was still out there somewhere.

THREE
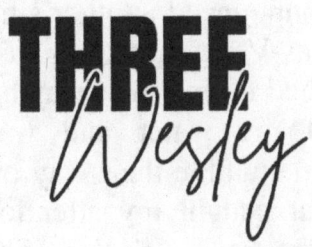
Wesley

Holy shit! I don't know what the hell had gotten into me, grabbing her like that. I was lucky she didn't kick me square in the balls. But damn, it was worth it. Even if I'd only gained a few minutes of time with her. I'd been eyeing her all night. It was by sheer luck that I'd run into her…physically.

I watched her as she gave me a coy smile over her shoulder and walked away.

I straightened my shirt and adjusted my pants and went back to my table.

"Dude, there you are. I thought I was going to have to send the troops after you."

I glanced around and back at Daniel. "You *are* the troops. Nice looking out, though."

He slapped my back. "Hey, what are friends for?"

We stood shoulder to shoulder at a two-top pub table, people watching. Well, I was watching people. He was watching ass. We were both recovering from jet lag. I was on my way to bed when he'd had the genius idea to go out for drinks at midnight. We'd barely been on the ground from our eight-hour flight.

The DJ announced another singer, and I cringed. All the talent Las Vegas had at its disposal and none of them had managed to find their way here.

I sipped my water and watched three very beautiful women stumble their way on to the stage. But one in particular caught my attention. The one being dragged from the back. *It's her.* She was even more beautiful washed in multicolored lights than she was when I had her in my arms in that dingy hallway.

"Dude, that chick over there is fine as fuck," Daniel said as he nudged my side to get my attention. "Check her out."

If Daniel had a particular taste in women, I'd have bet my next paycheck he was talking about the brunette walking up to sing. *My* brunette. But he was also an equal-opportunity pussy chaser.

"The blonde standing alone three tables over. She has a hell of a rack on her."

I glanced to my left and saw the woman he was talking about. "Indeed." I turned my attention back in front of me. She did have a hell of a rack, but she had nothing on dark-haired woman on stage. The one who I already knew smelled soft and sweet, like coconut and vanilla, and molded perfectly in my arms. The only thing I didn't know was how her naked body would feel wrapped around mine, or how every inch of her would taste on my tongue. Unfortunately, I'd never know.

Thankfully, they'd picked a short song. I watched as the three of them hurried off stage, back to their table, practically carrying each other, giggling like teenaged girls.

"I'm gonna go hit up the hottie with the big tits before she leaves, or someone gets her. Wish me luck."

"Luck? Do you need luck now?"

"No, not really." He disappeared into the crowd across the room heading for her table.

If I were *that* guy, I would have been right behind Daniel, hitting up the hot brunette for *her* number. Just because I didn't do it, didn't meant the thought hadn't crossed my mind a hundred times since I'd taken a risk letting her go once already.

Instead of chasing her down, I checked my phone. It was the same as always—a dozen spam and work emails, stock market updates, and an unexpected text from...*Ashley*? Asking me to please call her so we could talk. She was the last person I wanted to talk to, but I knew I could only blow her off for so long before she found a way to reach me. Oh, well. Not tonight.

Daniel came back in record time, even for him. "That was fast."

"No luck," he said. "She's already gone."

"Damn. So sorry about your loss." *And mine.*

"No loss, my friend. I'm not leaving this town without a hook-up. Believe me."

The bar slowly thinned out. I leaned into the table, watching as everyone dispersed.

"You all right?"

"I'm fine. I'm tired as hell and it's hot as balls in here." I checked my watch. "It's almost four. Time for me to call it a night, or morning. You forget, I still have

36

a half marathon to run in a lot less time than I care to admit. Here." I pulled out a couple of twenties and handed them to him. "For my tab. I'm going up to the room to go to bed."

"Dude, you drank water all night. You don't have a tab."

"Then give it to our waitress for putting up with your ass all night."

♡♡♡

"So, what are your plans for the day?" I asked Daniel, who was recovering from his beverage choices all night. Ten hours of travel on almost no sleep mixed with a few cocktails catches up to you quick. He'd learn one day, but not today.

"Well, when I finally decide to get out of bed I'll probably grab some food and head to the indoor pool. There's not much else to do since everything's blocked off for the race."

I tied my shoes and stood up. "Woah."

"Man, you look like shit. You okay?"

I took in a deep breath and slowly exhaled while the room spun. "Yeah, just got a headrush. It's all good. I'm going downstairs and grabbing a late lunch, then probably walk part of the Strip. Text me if you wanna catch up before the race, otherwise I'll just see you whenever I get back."

"Sounds like a plan, just be careful. You look a little pale."

"I said I'm fine, just stood up too fast."

37

♡♡♡

"Dr. Miller," Dr. Jones said as we shook hands. "How are you feeling today?"

"Like shit, but I'm still alive, so I guess I can't complain too much." I mean, what good would it do anyone to complain? There were people in far worse condition than me, most who would probably never make it through to tell about it, or worse, live an all-suffering life.

"I can appreciate your optimism. I looked over your labs and X-ray this morning; so far things are status quo. So, no news is good news, at this point. We're all just waiting."

Waiting. That's all I've done is wait since this disaster started a few years ago. "Right. No news is good news. Just waiting."

"It's unfortunate your health took a downturn, but that also works in your favor, you know? Sort of moves you up the list and gets things going a little faster."

"Yup." All I had to do was sit around and wait for some poor unfortunate soul to kick the bucket and hope we were a match.

"I'll keep a close eye on things and, of course, you'll know something as soon as I do."

"Appreciate it, Doc. You know where I'll be." I adjusted the oxygen tubing on my nose and took a few deep breaths. It felt good to breathe comfortably on my own.

Several months ago I was healthy, or so I thought, living a completely normal life working as an emergency room intensivist, going on daily runs by the river, banging my smokin' hot girlfriend, which I hadn't done in almost two months. Then poof life as I knew it went up in smoke in a matter of seconds. One minute I'm playing co-ed softball, thinking about what I'm going to cook for dinner, and the next thing I know I'm waking up in an ICU at my own damned hospital.

Dr. Jones left the room. He said something to someone in the hallway right outside my door. My brother, Warren, walked in. "Feel like company?"

"Always, since I'm now confined to this lovely crib." I gave one of the siderails of the bed a light shake.

He walked around the foot of the bed and sat in the chair by the window. "I saw Dr. Jones out there," he said, nodding towards the door. "What'd he have to say? Anything good?"

"Good as in they're ready to rush me off to the operating table and fix this fucking mess? No. We're still just waiting."

"Here, maybe this will help pass some of the time." He pulled a rolled-up magazine out of his back pocket and handed it to me.

"Playboy?"

"Even better. It's the latest issue of Business Trading.*"*

"Perfect. You know me, I always enjoyed jerking off to the stock market." I took a sip of water, appreciative of the fact that I wasn't intubated and still allowed to eat and drink...for now. "Speaking of jerking off, you haven't heard anything from Ash today, have you? I tried calling and texting but haven't gotten a

response yet." She tried to come by at least once a day to visit since visitors weren't allowed to spend the night. I figured, if nothing else, she'd be here by the end of the day.

"No. But I talked to Dad on the way here. He was heading over to your place to drop some food off or some shit for her so she wouldn't have to worry about not eating a home-cooked meal."

I laughed. "She hates cooking, so I'm sure she's been living on take-out now that her personal chef is laid up on his deathbed."

He huffed and turned serious. "Cut the deathbed pity-party shit, Wes. You are not on your deathbed."

I sat up and leaned towards him. "Really? Who's the one in denial about me now? We fucking knew this day might come. All those surgeries I had in the last two years were just me buying time and guess what? Time is up, brother. And if I don't get a match soon, however long soon is, you'll be planning my funeral next."

FOUR
Rowan

"Oh. My. God. Whose idea was it to go out last night?" I moaned as I covered my head with the pillow. I *knew* drinking all night was a bad idea, but I was grateful that Katie remembered to close the big-ass wall of curtains before we crawled into bed.

"I don't know," Kat said, "but I'm blaming Chloe for all of it. All. Of. It."

"Sounds like a plan to me."

We'd carted each other up to the room and stumbled into bed sometime after three in the morning. The bar was still in party mode, but we were not. Plus, Kat and I still had to run a half marathon in...I didn't know how long because I had no clue what time it was, and I was scared to look.

"My head is freaking pounding," I told Kat through my pillow. "I'm not running tonight. Just go without me."

She yanked the pillow off my head. "Oh, no. The hell you aren't. We didn't come all this way for you to crap out on me because of a few drinks."

I had no argument, so I rolled out of bed, and tiptoed into the master suite to check on Chloe. Of course, she was sound asleep, her curly hair a tangled mess, black silk eye mask over her eyes, mouth wide open. I debated on snapping a picture of her but closed the door and headed to the bathroom instead.

Yikes. My "beach wave" hair was everywhere but where it should have been and looked almost like Chloe's rats' nest of bedhead. Mine was just longer and darker, with less curl and a lot more frizz. My mascara was smeared halfway across my face.

I peeled off my dress, balled it up, and inhaled the sweet aroma soaked into the fabric. It still smelled like *him*.

♡♡♡

It took all of us until late afternoon to finally pull ourselves together and leave the suite. Our first stop was a restaurant on the main floor to load up on the healthiest carbs possible in an effort to ward off any lingering hangover. Chloe, of course, rubbed it in that she wasn't running, and ate the biggest bowl of spaghetti I'd ever seen.

"I don't know how you do it," I said to her. "You eat like trash and look like a model." For as long as I'd known her, she's resembled a tiny Barbie. A sassy, smart-mouthed Barbie. I don't think she'd ever weighed more than a hundred pounds.

"Genetics, I guess," she said with a mouth-full of food.

"We need to be checked into the race soon," Kat said as Chloe shoveled pasta into her mouth. "What are you gonna do for the rest of the afternoon?"

"Not sure yet. I'll probably just lounge around the indoor pool, go see my friend Louie, or maybe hit up the spa. Hell, I might do all three. I already checked and the spa is open twenty-four hours." Chloe was going to be living the life of luxury while Kat and I pounded pavement for thirteen miles. Though, we'd also be at the after-party at the finish line, and Chloe wouldn't have access. I felt bad she wouldn't be there with us.

After our late lunch / early dinner, we walked Chloe to the indoor pool, parted ways, then headed to the race check-in table.

"Well," Kat said as she secured her number to the front of her shirt, "ready or not, there's no turning back now."

"Oh, there is," I laughed. "But come hell or high water I will finish this race because I'll never hear the end of it if I don't. That and I've committed myself to a Bavarian cream donut as a reward for when we finish."

"I'm so there."

We stood with our group of runners watching the countdown clock. The first two groups of runners had already gone, and we were last to go. Las Vegas Boulevard had turned into a circus. We were surrounded by entertainment of the weirdest kind. People were dressed in a thousand variations of Elvis and some were in bikinis. Bikinis! Who the hell ran wearing only a bikini? All I could think was what if they fell? I did not want to imagine the pain of that road rash. And almost everyone was wearing something neon, glittery, or light-up...including Kat. Though she did look ridiculously cute in her hot pink attire and blinking headband. I chose the much safer route and went with all black—black tank top, black leggings, and matching shoes.

Then, I smelled something sexy. It was *him*. *No way*. My mind was playing tricks on me. I scanned the crowd as best as I could without being too obvious that I was trying to hunt down the man wearing that delicious scent.

"Looking for someone?" A deep voice close to my ear sent a chill down my spine, causing goosebumps along the way. As much as I'd like to have blamed it on the weather, it was most definitely not due to a sudden drop in temperature.

Traitorous body.

I looked over my shoulder and scanned him from head to toe, then back up again. Yup, there was no denying it was him. I stifled a cough, practically choking on my own spit. "What? No. I-I was just…" What in the hell was I doing? Besides making an ass of myself in front of probably one of the hottest men I'd ever laid eyes on.

He stepped up next to me, standing so close I could feel the tickle of the hairs on his arm brushing up against mine. The warmth of his body radiated against my side. "Well, whatever you *were* just doing," he said with a smirk, as he tugged at my ponytail. "good luck."

"Um, thanks. You too."

He smiled, then turned his focus straight ahead, giving me the perfect opportunity to study him—his clean-shaven face, dark eyes, and the strong outline of his jaw. I wanted to reach out and touch him, to feel his skin beneath my fingertips. But there was something about him, aside from his picture-perfect features, that I couldn't quite put my finger on. Something seemed *off*. So, me being Miss Smooth as Chunky Peanut Butter, blurted out of nowhere, "Are you feeling okay? You don't look so hot. I mean, you do, but not like that." The words came out before my filter engaged.

He flashed a smile at me that could have caused any woman's panties to drop. Smug bastard. He rolled his shoulders—his smooth, bare, sexy, shoulders. "Yeah, I'm feeling all right. Nerves, I guess. This your first marathon?"

"Yes, it's my first, last and only half," I corrected him. "I'm not going for the gusto. You?"

"Same—well, I'm only running the half, but it won't be my last."

Someone squeezed my hand, breaking my attention from Mr. Too Perfect for His Own Damned Good. "You ready?" Kat asked.

I nodded. "Definitely." Kat was squished into my other side and had hopefully missed the entire exchange between me and McHottie.

"Well, guess I'll see you at the finish line," he said. *Or not.* I had to get the hell away from him…whoever he was because I never asked him his name.

The air horn blared as the countdown clock hit zero. Flames of fire shot from the ballast that stretched over Las Vegas Boulevard. A DJ played some mix of funky techno and rap music as lasers danced through the sky and down across the runners. Finally. The last thirteen miles I'd ever run, then I'd be moving on to a new form of therapy that didn't involve strenuous physical activity.

I pressed forward, focusing on the finish line and my reward donut, trying not to allow myself to get distracted by *him*, wherever he was.

Runners had dwindled down to a few stragglers— a couple beside me, but most in front of me. I easily spotted Kat who had gotten ahead of me as usual.

My momentum tapered off as we passed the nine-mile mark. I gave myself a mental fist pump. If I held my pace, I'd be throwing myself to the ground at the finish line in under thirty minutes.

Then someone yelled behind me. "Help! Someone help!"

Immediately, I stopped running as my heartbeat doubled. I stood in the middle of the road as people jogged past me, turning their heads to see what was going on behind them.

There are no words to describe the sensation that takes over your entire body when you hear someone yell the words *help*. Help could mean a million things. *Help, I've fallen, and I can't get up! Help, someone's choking!* But for me, I knew from the tone in the voice of the person yelling that something was wrong. Very, very wrong.

But nothing could have prepared me for what I saw when I turned around.

FIVE

Rowan

Tears stung my eyes and threatened to fall, blurring the scene in front of me. Memories I fought so hard to block out came crashing against my chest like the weight of the waves of an angry ocean. All the oxygen had been sucked out of my lungs, leaving me gasping for air.

"We need help!"

Those words shook something in me, and I took off running toward the small group of people standing around the man on the ground. I fell to my knees beside him.

There were people around us, yet we were alone. Just me and him as he laid still on the blacktop.

"Do something!" someone yelled over my jumbled thoughts. "Are you a doctor or a nurse?"

No. I wanted to tell him. *No.* I'm not a fucking nurse.

I swallowed hard. "Yes. Yes. I'm a nurse."

Without any more thinking, I kicked it into high gear, letting the skills I'd spent years learning and practicing take over. "Has anyone checked for a pulse?"

"No. I don't think so." I pressed my fingers to his neck.

Nothing.

Come on, come on, come on. Shit!

This man was way too young to just collapse and die.

Techno-dance music blared as neon lights and lasers flashed bright patterns over us.

I leaned down and held my ear against his mouth.

"I need the medics! Now! Has anyone called nine-one-one? Someone get me a fucking AED!"

"Yes. We called. They're on the way." There was two people kneeled down across from me. They looked just as scared shitless as I felt inside. I could only imagine the look on my face. *Don't fuck this* up, I kept telling myself over and over. Don't. Fuck. This. Up.

I'd wasted too much time. I laced my fingers together, placed my hands on the middle of his chest and started pumping up and down. I counted and pumped.

I needed help.

Finally, someone said, "I know CPR. Let me help."

I kept pumping on his chest. "You're taking over, get ready. Now!" I pulled back, and the man beside me flew into place. I stumbled backward, landing on my ass, then forced myself to stand up. As soon as I was upright, fatigue assaulted me. I bent down, balancing myself with my hands on my thighs. I stared down with tunnel vision on that lifeless man lying in the middle of Las Vegas Boulevard.

"There's still no pulse."

Time ticked in slow motion as the medics arrived. They quickly pushed the bystanders out of the way and got to work. All at once they strapped an oxygen mask to his face, cut off his shirt, and stuck Zoll pads to his chest.

I watched as they worked hard and fast.

In all the chaos, I noticed a huge scar on his chest.

"He's in V-tach."

I watched the green lines on the black monitor. One hundred and eighty times per minute.

A robotic voice announced, *Shock advised, stand clear.*

"Charging. Everybody clear!"

His body jolted from the shock.

I closed my eyes as my knees slammed against the blacktop.

One of them shouted, "I got a pulse! Let's go!"

I sat back on my heels as they lifted him up, strapped him to the gurney and loaded him into the back of an ambulance.

All I could do was stare helplessly in a daze as the ambulance drove away.

♡♡♡

"Rowe, I'm so sorry I wasn't there for you," Kat said apologetically as she handed me a steaming cup of fresh coffee. She'd been so focused on running and pacing herself, always just a few steps ahead of me, that she'd never heard a thing. I couldn't blame her though. We'd agreed since the beginning that if we were separated at any point, we would just keep trudging forward and meet up at the finish line. That's exactly what she did, she kept moving forward.

"Thanks for the coffee. I'm glad at least one of us finished." I leaned up and took a sip from my cup, appreciating her gesture.

"You're welcome. I wish you could have, but someone else needed you more."

"Right." Someone needed me more and he was probably dead because of me. "Sorry you had to sleep on the couch. What time is it, anyway?"

"It's not a problem. The couch is actually comfortable. And it's just after one. I didn't want to wake you—you thrashed around that bed all night."

"One? In the afternoon?"

"Yup." She clicked on the bedside light and sat down on the bed next to me. "You wanna talk about it?"

"No, I don't want to talk about it. Not now, or ever. I need to take a shower." What I really wanted to do was just forget about the entire night. "Where's Chloe? Does she know what happened?"

"She's at the pool now, probably downing her second...or fifth mimosa. I'm not even sure what time she got back, but she was out pretty late. I told her about everything this morning." Kat squeezed my thigh through the covers. "I'm gonna join her downstairs in a bit if you wanna come down?"

"Let me see how I feel first. What I really want is to find that donut shop."

"That isn't a bad idea," she said as she stood and stretched. "I'm sorry I wasn't there for you."

"It's not your fault. You did what we agreed we'd do if we were separated." I set my coffee on the nightstand and headed for the shower. I was still wearing my running clothes.

My body ached from head to toe. I had abrasions on both of my knees and the palms of my hands were covered in road rash. I stripped out of my clothes, turned the shower on full steam, and stepped under the rainwater showerhead.

"Rowe," Kat said when I finally came out of the bathroom wrapped in a towel, my hair dripping wet. "We need to talk. There's been a slight change of plans."

"What, Kat? What's there to talk about?" I snipped at her without meaning to. "A man collapsed, went into cardiac arrest, and was sent to the hospital probably to die. All because of me. Is that what you want to talk about?"

"Rowe. He's not dead." Her words were soft and sweet.

My mind worked overtime processing what she said. "What do you mean he's not dead? How do you know?"

She pulled me to sit down on the bed. "Take a deep breath, Rowan. Breathe. One of the medics called you while you were in the shower."

"How? I-I don't…"

"Apparently at some point when they were getting ready to leave for the hospital you just kept frantically repeating your name and phone number to one of the paramedics. He wrote it down with a promise to call and give you an update as soon as he could." She looked down at the piece of paper in her hand. "His name is Evan Barterro. He went by the hospital this morning when he got off work." She handed me the paper from a hotel notepad that had Evan's name and number on it. "He said to call him if you have any questions...and to tell you Wesley is doing okay."

"Wesley?" Wesley! He had a name, and it was perfect. "Thank you, Kat." I sat clutching the tiny piece of paper, staring at Evan's name and number.

"Come on," she said, standing up, holding out her hand for me. "Let's get you dressed. We'll go pay Wesley a visit."

Wait, what? I looked at her like she had lost her damn mind. "Kat, I love you and all, but there is no way in hell."

"Don't you think today, of all days, is the day you let that shit go and don't look back. David has been gone for a year, and it just so happens you saved a man's life on damned near that same day one year later. If that isn't a sign or some form of redemption, I don't know what is."

I sniffled and wiped my nose on my towel. "Okay. You're right. Let's go. Just let me get a damned donut first, please."

"Thank you." She walked away and came back a few seconds later with a donut in her hand. "I already got you covered." She handed me the most beautiful donut I'd ever laid my hungry eyes on. "I ran across the street when I got off the phone with Evan."

I snatched it from her and took a huge bite out of the cream-filled treat. "Oh my God. Thank you," I said with a mouth full of food as my eyes rolled back in pleasure.

♡♡♡

We headed downstairs to update Chloe on the latest news about Wesley. When we found her, she was laid back in a chair near the edge of the pool. She popped up as we approached her.

"It's about time. Where are your swimsuits?"

"actually, we're heading to the hospital for a bit, first," Kat told her, then gave her the rundown on the phone call this morning and our plans to go see him.

"Really? Do y'all want me to go?"

Kat looked to me for the answer. I just shrugged. "Not unless you just want to? You look like you're pretty settled in here." She had a huge tote bag stuffed with God only knew what, towels, a Bluetooth speaker and a pitcher of juice set up on a side table. "Plus, that's a lot of shit. I'm not moving it."

Chloe shrugged, holding up a glass of juice.

"Mimosa?"

"Only in my cup. Orange juice in the pitcher, two bottles of champagne in my bag."

I laughed. "Wow. Stay and enjoy yourself. At least one of us has to get the most out of this vacation."

"Suit yourself." She laid back in her lounge chair and sipped her orange drink. "You know where I'll be."

"We'll be back in a little bit."

"I'll text you when we get back if you're not already in the room," Kat told her as we walked away.

53

We left Chloe at the pool and made our way to the circular driveway at the main entrance where an Uber was already waiting for us.

She looked over at me. "I knew if I didn't have one ready, you'd try to bail." She grabbed my hand and pulled me into the car.

I cursed her under my breath for knowing me so well.

Not ten minutes later, I found myself standing in the middle of the cold and barren rotunda of University Medical Center in Las Vegas, wishing I'd never taken up running.

"You can do this."

"I guess I kind of have to. You practically dragged me here." Even though I'd already decided on the ride over that I wasn't going to allow myself to make any more excuses. Seeing Wesley was all about getting closure.

We approached the help desk, and a plump gray-haired lady looked up at us over her gold-rimmed glasses. "Hi, how can I help you young ladies?"

"We're looking for Wesley Miller," Kat said. "He was brought here last night by EMS. From the race."

"Okay, give me just a minute." Her wrinkly fingers worked fast on the keyboard as she focused on the computer screen. "Ah, here he is." She scrunched her eyebrows together and adjusted her glasses.

I held my breath and waited for the worst possible news.

"Is something wrong?" Kat asked the old woman.

"Oh, no. Nothing's wrong. The old eyes just aren't what they used to be. Your friend is in the ICU. Visits are limited to two family members at a time, twice per day, one hour each visit. Are either of you two family?"

"Actually, yes," Kat said, wrapping her arm around mine. "She's family."

I nudged her side. *What in the hell was Katie about to get me into?*

After giving her our names and some questioning and a driver's license check, she finally handed us two sticker ID's. "So, family it is. Next visiting time starts in ten minutes."

I peeled the backing off the sticker and placed it over my left chest. "I have no idea where we're going."

Kat looked at her sticker badge before putting it on. "ICU – 213."

The air around us was cool and dry. It smelled like plastic, bleach, and sterility. The shiny floors reflected fluorescent lights with each step we took. We found the elevators and took one to the second floor. Once the doors opened, we followed the signs on the walls and wound our way around to the double doors labeled *Intensive Care Unit 200 - 230.*

My heart pounded.

The double doors to the ICU hallway opened with a loud *BANG*, causing us both to practically jump out of our skin and laugh. "Okay, that's our sign," I said. "Let's go."

We walked down a long corridor, and a second set of doors labeled *Family Waiting* opened into a huge, carpeted room with an unoccupied help desk, and a sign that read: "Please check in." I followed the prompts on the screen, hoping it wouldn't ask me for any personal information about the patient, otherwise I was screwed.

Thankfully, I made it through the second check-in process, and then we sat on the far side of the room and waited. There were at least twenty other people, all waiting to see their loved ones.

After what felt like an eternity, a nurse in green scrubs, holding a clipboard opened a door on the other side of the room. "I need the family members of Alston, Garza, Lopez, Miller, and Porter. Please remember, visits are limited to two people at a time and one hour. You're welcome to rotate family members if you'd like." A few people stood and walked towards the nurse.

A wave of nausea rushed over me. "Rowan, you look like shit. Are you okay?" Kat asked.

I gave myself an internal pep talk, trying not to lose my donut. "Yeah, I'm fine. Indigestion."

The nurse looked up from her clipboard and called out a little louder, "Are the families of Garza or Miller here?" There was a small group of people crowded around the door, looking at me, no doubt wondering what the holdup was and if this delay would cut into their visiting hours.

"That's you," Kat said. "Come get me if you need me. I'll be right here. Plus, *Judge Judy* is on."

"Thank you." She knew how much all of this meant to me and no matter how much I needed her, there were some things I needed to face on my own…*like him.*

All eyes were on me as I approached the group. "Miller," I said to the nurse. She wrote something on the paper in front of her.

"Okay, guys," she said as she tapped her name badge on a black box on the wall and pulled the door open. "Follow me."

The small group of people moved along like they all knew exactly where they were going. I must have looked lost because a hand touched my arm. "Seventh door on the right." I turned and saw the nurse with her clipboard walking off in a different direction. I had half a mind to follow her.

All of the rooms looked just like every other ICU. The walls facing the hallway weren't really walls. They were floor-to-ceiling glass panels that opened like a huge accordion, with pastel rainbow-colored curtains that expanded the entire glass section from the floor to the ceiling.

The numbers on the wall increased by two as I took my time getting to the seventh door on the right. Room 213.

I froze outside of his room. It was so hard to just *move*. I didn't know this guy from Adam, and I'd only learned his name a little while ago. Maybe because knowing his name made him real. It made him a person, someone I'd made a very physical connection with, and not just another victim. I could have walked away and never laid eyes on him or his face, again, and never know the outcome of his life. He wouldn't even have known I was here to see him except for my name on a sheet of paper that I had no doubt in my mind would be in the shredder by the end of the day.

The curtain in front of his room flung back, causing me to jump. My hand shot up to my cover my mouth, stifling a yelp.

It was a nurse. "Sorry, didn't mean to scare you. Are you here to see Mr. Miller?"

"Um, yeah. I guess I am."

"Come on in. He's pretty out of it. But he's been responding to me off and on. I'll be back in a bit to check on him."

I stepped into the room and laid eyes on him for the first time since last night. Despite the IV line in his neck and various tubes tethering him to a pole, he looked peaceful. His dark hair was disheveled, and he was beyond a five-o'clock shadow. But his features were soft and relaxed. His breathing was even and unlabored. A ventilator sent a *tss* of air down a blue tube through his mouth, into his lungs; his chest rising and falling with each *tss*. The heart monitor hanging on the wall over the bed gave off a steady rhythm; a perfect sixty-two times per minute. It beat the hell out of the one eighty he was throwing the last time I saw him.

The nurse came back into the room, and I was still standing in the same spot she'd left me five minutes ago. "Sorry, I'm just gonna give him some pain meds. See if we can get that blood pressure down a little bit." She said something to him, then asked me, "You doin' okay in here?"

"Yeah, I'm good. Thanks." Fucking peachy. I folded my arms across my chest into a hug. "Why is he on the ventilator?"

"It's just supplemental to let his lungs rest. He's got pneumonia. And with his cardiac history, he just needs some time to recover."

Cardiac history. That explained the scar.

I had so many questions that only he could answer, but never would. And unfortunately, the whole patient protection law prevented her from telling me too much information. My stomach sank. "Do you think he'll need it long? The vent?"

She smiled. "Honestly, there's no way to know. We'll watch his vitals, and the doctor will probably have respiratory start weaning him off the vent this afternoon and see how he does. Doc likes to do things pretty quick."

"Thank you. I guess that's all."

"You're welcome. Let me know if you need anything else. You still have about forty-five minutes left to visit." She walked out and drew the curtain shut behind her.

All of the thoughts that paralyzed me vanished. Instead of worrying about unanswered questions, I grabbed the only chair in the room, slid it across the floor and scooted it as close to the bed as I could get, and sat down beside him. Without even thinking, I lowered the bedside railing, laid my head against his shoulder, and hugged his arm into my chest as I held his hand. It felt like the best thing to do for him, and for me.

Then, out of nowhere, I poured my heart out and started talking to him. It's what I always told my patients' family members to do. *We don't know if they can hear you. Just talk.*

"Wesley." I paused and took a few deep breaths. "I don't know if you can hear me right now, but I'm here. I'm Rowan, and well, you scared the shit out of me in more ways than one. You took my breath away when you literally caught me from hitting the floor, and then again when you collapsed." Tears streamed from my eyes. "Honestly, I don't know if we'll ever see each other again, but I want you to be okay. I want you to get out of here and run more marathons. Hell, run a few for me because I'm done running. I want you to get out of here and live your best life, Wesley Miller."

Ironic. I told him to go out live his best life, when in reality I couldn't even follow my own advice. I'd been stuck in the past for so long, I let it keep me from moving forward.

I rubbed his arm, the one that brushed against me that sent chills to my core, and for the first time in so long, I appreciated what it felt like to be physically close to a man. What it felt like to touch his skin; the sensation of the soft hairs of his arms beneath my fingertips; the feel of his fingers laced with mine. I knew he wasn't mine to touch, but I was here, and he needed me. Selfishly, I needed him.

Something crashed to the floor, and I jolted upright.

"Mrs. Miller, it's been an hour. Visiting time is over," his nurse said as she scanned a bag of IV medication.

"Sorry, I guess I fell asleep. Please take care of him."

I looked at his hand, fingers still woven with mine. As I stood up to leave, I planted a soft kiss on his forehead. He was warm and he was alive.

"Well, how'd it go?" Katie asked when I got back to the waiting room. She was flipping through a *US Weekly*, eating a Honey Bun.

"It went fine." Better than I could have ever imagined.

"So, what happened? He gonna be okay?"

"I think so. He's got pneumonia. He should recover pretty quick." It was so much more than that, but I wasn't ready to tell her about his cardiac history because I didn't know enough about him to tell her.

"Damn, that's it? Just pneumonia? Poor guy almost got taken out by a respiratory virus? Damn."

She peeled back the wrapper on her pastry and took another bite out of it.

"Really?" I pointed at the sticky treat. "You're ridiculous."

"I'm making up for last night. Plus, I didn't get to eat *my* donut this morning unlike someone, or lunch before we left." She tossed the magazine down on the table beside her.

"Come on, then." I grabbed her hand and pulled her up to stand. "Let's go get some food and find Chloe before she blows her annual income on more Louis."

SIX
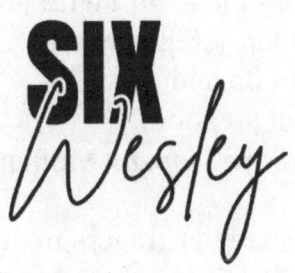
Wesley

Ho-ly shit. My chest was on fire. And my head. *Wow*. My ass was numb. *Why is my ass numb?* Good God, that motherfucking beeping. What *was* that?

I tried to swallow, but something was blocking my throat. What t*he fuck?* I was intubated? I was motherfucking intubated. *Okay, calm down, Wes, think for a minute. Think. Think. You are…*not where I was the last time I remembered being somewhere. There was no way I was back in the hospital. I started to wonder if someone had slipped me a roofie. That this was all a dream, or I was now part of an organ harvesting ring. *Shit*, I sure as hell hoped not. I couldn't afford to lose any more vital organs.

I tried moving, but my body was like lead.

"Do you think he'll need it long?" I heard a voice say. The voice was angelic and soft and beautiful…and scared. Someone in the distance responded with something about vitals and sedation. I thought I was done being the patient.

Then the voice I loved to hear got closer. "Thanks, that's all I needed to hear."

Something made an awful sound as it slid across the floor, and then I felt a hand... Her hand? It slowly caressed my arm up and down.

God it felt so good.

Come on eyes, open! Mother. Of. God. I was *so* sleepy.

She threaded her fingers in mine as she pulled my arm against her. I felt her head rest on my shoulder. Her hair was so close I could smell her shampoo. She smelled sweet and so familiar. Then recognition hit. It *was* her. It was the woman from the club. Fucking hell, I'd died and gone to heaven. I swear, if this was real, if *she* was here, I'd never do anything stupid again, ever. I'd make up with Van Buren. I'd even start going to church. Okay, maybe not, but I'd do better in life.

I could feel her soft hair against my collarbone, just begging me to run my hands through it. But I couldn't move. I was a worthless sack of leaden flesh.

If I ever came out of this state, I was going to do everything within my power to find her.

"Wesley," she said.

Yes? I'm here.

"I don't know if you can hear me, but I'm here."

I can hear you. Please don't leave.

"I'm Rowan, and well, you scare the shit out of me in me more ways than one."

Rowan...Rowan? That was all I'd ever need to hear.

Then, her voice faded as I drifted back off to la-la land.

♡♡♡

"Dr. Miller, how are you feeling?"

That was a loaded question, considering I'd recently had my chest sawed open, but I was alive, so that's something. After a few weeks of waiting, I'd finally gotten the news I wanted—no, needed—to hear. They had a match. "About as good as can be."

"Well, you can expect a lot of pain, but don't let it get out of hand. If you need anything for it, call me."

"Sure thing, thanks."

When my nurse left the room, I looked over at the sexy blonde sitting in the chair across the room.

She looked up from her phone and smiled at me. "I'd ask how you're feeling, but I think you already answered that."

"Come here," I said to her. "I've missed you."

She stood and walked up beside my hospital bed. "I missed you too."

"Good. Feels good to finally be awake. You okay?"

"Yeah. Just hoping we can put this behind us and get back home soon. I'm sick of being in the hospital."

"Ha. You?" I looked down at the twelve-inch bandage on my chest. "Me too."

She checked her phone again.

"Someone important?" I wasn't trying to be an asshole, but after everything I'd been through, the least

she could have done was give me two minutes of her undivided attention.

"Just Kels. She wants to know when I'm going to be home."

"Yeah, Kels. Just go, Ash. Obviously, I'm not going anywhere."

"You sure? I can stay longer if you want."

"Nah. I'm going to take them up on their offer and get something for pain and go back to sleep."

"Okay. I'll come back tomorrow." She bent down, kissed my forehead, grabbed her purse off the chair, and left.

I watched my girlfriend of five years walk away like it would be the last time I was going to see her. Things between us had changed over time, even more so once I was put on the transplant list. I'd finally had a fair shot at a healthy life again, and she seemed to pull away all the same.

Bits and pieces of information replayed in my mind like an old-timey movie, but in the distance, as I laid in the hospital bed trying to figure out how I managed to get here, again.

The dizzy spells were back. I checked my pulse a few times. Nothing out of the ordinary there. I felt warm and jittery but shook it off and made a mental note to follow up with my primary when I got home. I'd say I needed to lay off the drugs, but that wasn't my style. Then the race. Okay, I'd made it that far. I was running, and *oooh,* there she was.

Woah! Who turned on the lights? I managed to crack my eyelids, but it was way too bright. Would hospitals ever learn to use indirect lighting?

"Wesley?" I heard a voice. "If you can hear me, squeeze my hand."

No. Get this godforsaken tube out of my throat! Better yet just get me the fuck out of here.

"Give him a few minutes. Let the sedation wear off. I'll come back and check on him."

A new voice. *Wait, dude, where are you going?* I had questions and needed some answers, buddy.

"Wesley, squeeze my hand," the other voice demanded. Okay, fine. I felt fingers in my hand and gave them a squeeze. "Weak, but it's a start," she said.

Weak? I'll show you weak! Ask me again. Ask me again... But her hand was gone.

Hello? Still got a tube in my throat.

♡♡♡

I had no idea when I'd finally been extubated. It could have been yesterday or two weeks ago. All I knew was that I was about to get some damn answers. I swallowed hard, and as dry and sore as my throat was, it felt good all the same. At least I was still alive.

I sipped ice water as I listened to my doctor tell me about something I thought was long behind me. I could not believe what I was hearing.

"You have pneumonia and went into pulseless V-tach, lost consciousness, and collapsed during your race; the rest, as they say, is history. Thankfully, though, the

66

people around you responded pretty quickly, thanks to one fast-acting young lady who saved your life," Dr. Blackwell said to me matter-of-fact.

I was not used to being on this side of the whitecoat. I'd been the patient before, and I did not like it at all. One, I desperately needed to take a shower. Two, I was wearing a dress that was wide open in the back. Three, I was still peeing through a tube. Fucking pneumonia and these immunosuppressant drugs I'd be on for the rest of my life. This was just one of those risks, unfortunately, that came with an organ transplant.

"Yeah, I'm grateful," I told him. "How long have I been out, and how long are you going to keep me here?"

"You were only sedated and intubated for less than twenty-four hours," he said, looking down at his notes. "You aren't entirely out of the woods, you know that. But you're still relatively young and resilient. Give it another day or so. If you do okay tonight, I'll review your labs in the morning and see about getting you out of here before Wednesday. You can follow-up with your PCP."

I rubbed my face. God, I needed to shave, but it felt good to finally have that tube out of my throat. Now if they'd just get the ones out of my neck and dick, I'd be golden.

"Okay," I said, "I'll cooperate." Not like I really had a choice. It was a pain in the ass to leave AMA— against medical advice. No one wanted to do that paperwork, and insurance wouldn't pay out if I left. "Can I get some of these other tubes out of me?" I looked down.

"Of course." Dr. Blackwell stood and shook my hand. "Take care, Dr. Miller. We'll get that tube situation taken care of and I'll see you again before you leave."

"Yeah, thanks, Doc."

He turned and walked out. At least I had something to look forward to. I laid in bed and wondered what was going on at home, how the ER was doing without me, or if my brother knew where I was. Surely, he did. He wouldn't go this long without trying to contact me. And Daniel. Where was he?

My phone! Where was my cell? And my wallet? I hit the nurse call light and told the guy in the speaker I'd like my stuff since I still had strict orders for bed rest. A few minutes later, my nurse came in and pulled a clear belonging bag from a cabinet stuffed with my things and handed it to me.

"Has anyone been here?" I knew someone had been here, I just wanted confirmation it wasn't all just something I'd made up in my drugged state of mind.

"Of course. Your friend Daniel was here yesterday morning. He said he had to get back home and you'd understand, but he called earlier to check in on you. And your wife was here yesterday, too. I haven't seen her today unless she snuck in and I missed her."

My wife? That was rich considering I didn't have a wife. Rowan was the only female I remembered.

"I did find this stuck to the side of your bed. Thought you'd like to keep it."

She handed me a black-and-white name tag. Rowan Miller. *Miller? What the?* Oh. My. God. She used my last name to get into the ICU. *Ha!* But fuck, she was just as beautiful as I'd remembered, and she was here.

"Yeah, I'll keep it. Thanks."

"You're welcome. I'll be back and check on you in a bit. Call me if you need anything."

"Will do."

I dug through the bag and found my phone. Of course, it was dead. A small sheet of paper fell out. I recognized it immediately. It was my medical history and emergency contact list that I kept in my wallet. It wasn't much of a list though. My medical history was longer than my list of emergency contacts, since the only name on it was my brother, Warren.

Someone was here though…my *wife*? That made me laugh.

♡♡♡

"That's it. You're all set, Mr. Miller," the nurse said to me as she finished going over my discharge instructions. True to his word, Dr. Blackwell discharged me home as soon as he felt I was medically cleared. Halle-fucking-lujah.

"Transportation is on their way to come get you. Best of luck to you, Doctor. Take care, and I hope you find your girl."

"Thanks, me too." Come hell or highwater I was going to find her. While I waited for my ride downstairs, I called the hotel to check on my stuff, but Daniel had already taken everything home with him. My next call was to him to tell him thanks for looking out and I was being discharged. Then, my brother, Warren. I loved him because he was family, but man, the dude was uptight. I jokingly called him Mr. Personality because he was anything but that.

"Hey brother. How are you feeling?"

"Not too bad, considering. I'll be home this afternoon. Just pick me up from the airport. My plane lands at 19:28 tonight, your time."

"Sounds good. I'll see you then."

Short and to the point. We said our goodbyes, and I grabbed what few personal belongings I had with me just as a young man walked into the room pushing a wheelchair. You gotta be kidding me.

"Is that necessary?" I asked with a "give me a fucking break" look on my face.

He laughed. "Unfortunately, yes, sir, it is. Hospital policy."

SEVEN

Rowan

There really was no place like home.

After everything that happened in Vegas, I decided it was best to pay a visit to Dr. Holland before I changed my mind…again. I was sure he'd appreciate my willingness to visit with him, seeing as I flat-out cancelled our last two sessions without giving any sign of scheduling any more appointments.

Plus, I loved his office. He, or probably his wife, had set up it up cozy and homelike. It wasn't filled with stuffy leather furniture and ugly brass lamps, or shelves stocked with books filled with medical jargon. It was warm and comfortable and felt like home.

"Rowan," Dr. Holland said as he entered his office.

"Hi, Dr. Holland. How are you?"

He walked around his giant desk and grabbed a notepad. "Oh, I can't complain. I'm so glad you're here."

I stood up and shook his hand before he sat down in the chair across from the couch. "Yeah, thanks, me too."

"Please, have a seat. You know the drill." He waved his hand at the fluffy, overstuffed beige couch. I did not object. It was probably the most comfortable couch I'd ever sat on, plus there was the added bonus that he encouraged his patients to take off their shoes put their feet up on the coffee table. That was exactly how I planned to spend the next hour.

"So, tell me, how was your trip and race? Did you finish?"

"Something like that." I started at the beginning, unloading everything from the time we left Friday, running into Wesley, the race, to going to the hospital to see him. Sometimes, during our sessions, he jotted down notes, and other times he just doodled little pictures as he listened.

"Well..." I said pushing for his professional feedback.

"Well, what?" Would you like a response, or did you just need to offload onto me? Because we can go either way. You tell me what you want, Rowan."

I couldn't believe what I was hearing. He wasn't going into his drawn-out therapeutic advice sessions. He was making me decide? I didn't know what the hell I wanted, that's why I went to him. "Well, I want to know what you think. What should I do?"

He wrote something else down on his yellow pad. "Do about what specifically?"

"Dr. Holland. I didn't come here to info dump. I mean, I did, but I do that to my friends. I need your professional advice. Please."

"Okay, well, first let me say, I am proud of you and how far you've come in your journey. Rather than coming to me and possibly risk reopening your wound, you cancelled our session and went out on your own on the weekend of the one-year anniversary of your late fiancé's death. While part of it seems a little reckless, you held your own, and I wouldn't expect anything less of you. It seems as though you were exactly where you needed to be when you needed to be there. You saved another human's life, even though you also vowed to forever leave that role because you've always held yourself responsible for not being able to save David. But, like we've talked about, you've experienced a lot of death and trauma in your life. Where other matters are concerned, I think you've finally accepted David's death for what it was. An accident. Now you're moving forward and experiencing some guilt about it." The reality of everything he said hung thick in the air. He was right. I was moving forward with my life without David. After a few minutes, he broke the silence. "How about this? I want you to consider something for me, please."

"What's that?"

"Have you thought about reaching out to the agency who handled David's organ donation?"

I sank back into the couch and crossed my arms. "No. I have not. It's never once crossed my mind. For what?" For fuck's sake. This was not how I expected tonight to go. David being an organ donor was something I'd thought about almost every single day since he died. Not meeting the recipient part, but the fact that another living, breathing person was walking around with a vital organ from David's own flesh and blood. The thought brought me, oddly, some joy, that David's noble gesture was able to help save another person's life. But by the same token, it killed me that he had to die for it. All my hopes and dreams were ripped out from under me like a loose throw rug, so someone else could wake up to see another day.

"Maybe you should, Rowan. Reach out and see if you can meet one of the organ recipients—if there is more than one. That is if you want to, of course. It can be the last leg of your journey and closing this chapter in your life."

It felt like my healed wound had not only been ripped open, but someone had stuck a knife in it, twisting it back and forth, making sure it never healed.

The room-dividing curtain pulled back. "Ms. Honeycutt?" the nurse said as she approached my bed.

"Where is my fiancé?" I could barely get the words out. They'd been pumping me full of pain meds ever since EMS loaded me into the back of the ambulance. Everything hurt, and the room spun every time I tried to sit up.

"Ms. Honeycutt, I need you to lay down. Please. Stop trying to get up." The woman in blue scrubs put her hands on my shoulders and eased me back down to the bed. I didn't have the strength to fight her back.

"You didn't answer my fucking question," I yelled at her. "Where. Is. David? Where is my fiancé?" I

sobbed, she diverted. I knew the game very well; I'd played it myself a thousand times. Something was very wrong with him and with me. When I was awake, all I did was hurt all over and throw up.

The man on the other side of the curtain in the makeshift room next to me was screaming, "Man, someone shut that bitch up," to anyone who would listen to him, which, from experience, was no one.

"Ms. Honeycutt, please, listen to me. I need to ask you a question. How far along are you?"

"What? How far along with what?" What the fuck was she talking about? How far along am I?

She rubbed her hand down my arm trying to soothe me. I jerked away from her. "Your pregnancy. How far along are you? Do you know? I'm waiting for the on-call obstetrician to get here to examine you. He's on his way now."

Pregnancy? *I'm not...* Oh God.

Instinctively, I rubbed my hand over my stomach as I awoke. There were still no words to describe the hell I went through that night.

I tossed the covers back and sat in the middle of my bed in a cold sweat. Something had to give, or I was going to break. All I wanted at this point in my life was some routine. I needed normalcy. I took a sip of water from the glass on my nightstand and thought back to my session with Dr. Holland. His suggestion for me to try to contact one of David's organ recipients played on repeat.

The thought paralyzed me. Did I really want to meet some stranger walking around with one of David's vital organs knowing damn good and well David had to die for them? Did they know I lost everything that night? How could I even do it without feeling bitter towards them?

The laptop sitting on the desk at the foot of my bed taunted me. Eventually I caved. "Just get this shit over with," I said out loud to myself. It was after three in the morning and I had nothing better to do. The screen came to life and after a few minutes of searching, I found the contact email address of the agency that had handled David's case. I sat there at my dad's desk and started banging furiously on the keyboard, typing as anger rushed through my veins and words and tears flowed uncontrollably as I typed out a message to the agency and hit Save.

EIGHT

Wesley

Home. It was so nice to be home and getting back into my routine. I was pretty sure I'd never take for granted what it felt like to be a patient or still have my life or to be sleeping in my own bed. I was even grateful for Chicago's below-freezing temperatures. It meant I wasn't toes to the sky.

I also vowed to do whatever I needed to find the woman who not only played a huge role in saving my life but checked into the hospital as my wife so she could visit me. Real slick. I liked her even more for that reason alone. But locating her was going to be a royal pain in my ass because I didn't have a clue where she was from or have *her* last name.

"What about the race registration?" Daniel asked, kicking back in one of my office chairs, throwing his feet up on my desk.

"You're a slacker and a fucking genius." Daniel and I had worked together in the emergency department since residency, and we'd been friends even longer. I gave him a ton of shit, but he was a damn good doctor and a hell of a lot like a brother. "I don't know why I didn't think of that." I walked past him and threw his feet off my desk. I sat down and pulled up the race coordinator's information on my laptop. "I'm not sure they'll give me what I'm looking for though. Everyone is so damn worried about security and privacy these days." Hell, with all the stalkers and ease of access to information, I guess I couldn't blame them for being concerned; I was about to look like a stalker myself.

"Yeah, but you said her name is Rowan. How many Rowans do you think registered for that race? Even out of the tens of thousands of runners? Plus, you have a picture of her."

He had a very valid point. But that was all he had because as far as he was concerned, I was just looking for the woman who saved my life; he didn't know I'd already met her at the bar. What I needed more than anything was her real last name. Though, as much as I hated to admit it, *Rowan Miller* did have a very nice ring to it.

He leaned forward. "So, how did she find you at the hospital, anyway? Did you talk to her? I don't think you ever told me."

Shit. Didn't think that one through yet. "I didn't? I thought I told you?" I said, never taking my eyes off of my computer.

"Hmm, no, you didn't."

"I didn't actually talk to her, but one of my nurses confirmed her role in all of this and that she came to the hospital to see me. I'm just sorry I wasn't awake for her visit."

"Gotcha. So you don't know what she looks like? How the hell are you going to know you've even found her?"

"Trust me, I'll know. Now be quiet and let me work."

While Daniel stared at his phone, I searched Google and found a generic contact email address and shot a friendly email introducing myself, asking for a copy of the race registrants. If I could just get a list of first and last names, I'd be golden. Google would do the hard work, like figuring out what part of the country, or world, Rowan was from.

"Okay, sent," I said to Daniel. "Wish me luck."

He stood to leave my office. "Good luck, man, I hope you find her."

Me too. "Thanks. Oh, speaking of finding people, have you talked to that chick you hooked up with while I was on my deathbed?" It was half joke, half sarcasm, 100 percent truth. It wasn't his fault he wasn't at the race. Vegas was just a pit stop between Hawaii and home, and Daniel wasn't a runner. Hell, as far as he knew I was out all night at the after-party, until he'd talked to my brother the next morning.

"Nah, man. She was fun, but that was a one and done. Know what I mean?"

"I do. All of your women are 'one and done.'"

"Don't hate the player, hate the game."

"One of these days you're going to be too old for 'the game'. Is my brother still here?"

"Yeah, probably watching porn."

"Good. Tell him to come see me before he leaves."

"Will do." He left and shut the door as he exited my home office. I leaned back in my chair and threw my feet up on my desk. No one was allowed to do that but me. As I sat back and thought about the past couple of weeks, I'd never been more grateful to have my life saved—again—but the only thing I could see clearly through all my jumbled thoughts was *her* face. The way her long, dark hair felt between my fingers. How that black dress molded to her every curve. The look on her face when I caught her in my arms and how perfect she felt there. Those images and the feel of her body against mine would forever be burned into my memory.

My computer dinged with a new email. Between my regular time off, my trip to Hawaii and then Vegas, I'd missed almost three weeks of work and damned near maxed out the storage space in my inbox. Most of it was shit mail, but I checked the new one anyway.

Livy Benson. I had no idea who that was, but it looked legit. I opened it and hoped it wasn't a virus.

Hi Dr. Miller,

Thanks for reaching out about the race! I hope you're feeling better. We all heard about what happened. Taking into consideration your situation and request, I've attached a spreadsheet with every race participant whose first name starts with an R., along with their last name, and city and state provided for registration. Unfortunately, I cannot include first names. Please let me know if I can help you out in any other way.

Hope you join us next year so we can watch you finish the race!

Best of luck in your search,
Livy Benson
Rock 'N' Roll Marathon Coordinator

My heart pounded furiously inside my chest. I actually had a list of names, albeit last names, but it was a start, and more than I had an hour ago.

I opened the attachment and almost passed out. There were over two hundred people on the list whose first name initial was *R*. Two hundred fifty-seven to be exact. *Jesus*. This was going to take me for-fucking-ever. I could only hope she used her real first name because that was all I had.

I'd never, in over thirty years of life, sat down and written anyone a letter, much less one pouring my heart out to a total stranger. Rowan was going to think I was a psychopath when and if I found her. My hope was that this time the real Rowan would get my letter, read it, think it was sweet and, at the very least, call me so I could thank her personally for helping save my life.

After searching for her first name paired with a random last name and corresponding city from the list in a Google search, I'd written and sent at least five letters with my business card attached. I had no idea just how many Rowan's existed.

Searching for her was hard, even with the internet. Especially trying to find a person who apparently didn't have a single social media account. I held out some hope that I'd struck gold with the hit I got on a hospital in Memphis. When I typed Rowan Honeycutt, Memphis, TN, I got an exact match on the Memphis Regional Hospital website. I just wished there'd been a picture I could compare to the one on the name badge, or the image of her I'd burned to memory. But there wasn't. It was just a list of names. On the bright side, finding this Rowan's name for receiving an award for exceptional patient care and satisfaction—which was more than I could say for my ex, though *she* had the satisfaction part nailed down—was reassuring. Rowan at least had some integrity. I wrote a letter and sent it to her employer's HR department and waited.

There was a soft knock on my office door. "Come in," I called out without looking up from then never-ending stacks of papers spread out all over my desk in front of me.

"Dr. Miller, how are you?"

"Doc. Long time, no see." I stood up and outstretched my arm to shake his hand. "I'm about as good as can be, and better than most. How the hell are you? Have a seat." I gestured to the leather chairs in front of my desk.

We sat down. "Can't complain myself. Just finished up a case and wanted to come check in on you. How's the first day back at work treating you?"

"Same as usual. I'll probably spend the next month playing catch-up on emails alone. How'd surgery go?" *Thank God it wasn't mine.* Dr. Jones had been a colleague of mine for several years. He was also the cardiothoracic surgeon who'd performed my heart transplant. I was scared to death of a man capable of splitting open someone's chest and physically replacing one of their most vital organs. I also had the utmost respect for him because I was fortunate enough to be one of his most successful cases.

"Not to brag, but I expect her to have a full recovery. How's your ole heart doing since your vacation?"

"Man, this thing is ticking like a Timex. Thank you again. Hell, I can't thank you enough. For everything."

"Ah, it was nothing. I'm glad it's all well, Dr. Miller. It's been a year, you know? You're pretty much out of the clear for anything major at this point. Just take care of yourself and consider this our one-year follow-up." He let out a laugh, but I knew he was serious. Fine by me because, ironically, I hated going to the doctor.

"Thanks, man. I never thought I'd be one of your patients. I'm grateful, but it's still a little weird knowing someone had to lose their life just to save mine."

"We see it every day, Wes. I wouldn't wish this on anyone," he said as he stood to leave, "but sometimes we thank God for some strange things, even car wrecks."

NINE
Rowan

"Have you tried calling the hospital to check on him since we left?"

"Are you crazy? No I haven't called to check on him. I barely made it through the doors to go see him in the first place." Plus, the reality of Wesley's situation was, if he pulled through, he should already be home and getting on with his life. The human body is an amazing machine. It can endure all types of stress and illness and recover just the same as if nothing ever happened. I worried about him, though, but deep down, a part of me felt better off not knowing anything else about him. That didn't keep me from thinking about him non-stop. "We both know if everything went smooth, he should be home by now."

"Maybe so. Do you want me to do it?" she asked as she filled two cups with orange juice. If there was one thing I'd learned about Katie after spending so much time with her, it was that she was persistent and had a mixed drink for every occasion. "I'll call if you want me to. At least let me find out if and when he got discharged?"

"What difference would that make? I'd rather remember him how I last saw him and imagine him waking up and walking out of there. The less I know about him, the better off I am." I grabbed my glass of juice and gulped it down before she could add any champagne.

"Suit yourself," she said with a smirk. "But I know you, and I think deep down, you *need* to know. It's in your blood. And don't you think if he knew you went to visit him at the hospital, he'd want to keep in touch with the super-awesome female who saved his life?"

I shook my head. It didn't matter what he wanted. As far as he or I or anyone was concerned we were total strangers who, under weird circumstances, just happened to be at the right place at the right time. I never kept tabs on any of my other patients, and that's all he was ever going to be to me. "Not happening. The hospital isn't going to give you any information on him, anyway. Plus, this isn't a fairy tale, Kat. Just leave it alone."

"Fine. I'll change the subject. Have you thought about getting back into the dating scene now that you…you know?" Her voice trailed off.

"You can't be serious."

"Why not? You said once we got home you would—."

"I know what I said. What do you have up your sleeve, Kathryn McDonald? You're up to something, aren't you?"

She smiled. "Maaaybe."

"No. The thought has not crossed my mind literally one time." Because the only person I'd thought about since we got home, was *him*.

"Well, I might know someone."

"Katie!" I squealed. "Don't you dare try pulling some slick shit and set me up."

"Oh, come on! He's super cute, and he has a dog."

"A dog? Really? Well, that's a game changer. Sign me up, then. Twice!"

"Really? For real?"

"No! Not for real. I don't want you hooking me up on *one* blind date, much less two. I don't care if he has a whole dog rescue."

She took a sip of her mimosa and looked at me over the rim of her cup. "Too late."

I rolled my eyes but didn't have time to argue because my phone rang. "Saved by the bell. But this conversation isn't over."

"Hello?" I said as I answered the call. "This is she. I did? Is today good? Okay, I'll come get it shortly. Thank you. See you soon." I disconnected.

Kat looked at me like a hungry puppy waiting for food to drop on the floor. "Well? Who was that?"

"Wendy Roberson from human resources at Regional."

"Wendy? Was she offering you your job back?"

That made me laugh. "No, she didn't offer me a job. Nice try though. She said she received a letter addressed to me."

Kat raised an eyebrow. "A letter? Why would someone mail you a letter there?"

"I don't know. She offered to forward it here, but it'll be quicker just to go pick it up myself."

"Well, I'm clearly more curious than you, and a lot more impatient. Let's go." She stood and tossed me her keys. "You're driving."

We left our drinks on the counter and headed out the door. It was only a fifteen-minute drive to the hospital without traffic, and another five-minute walk between the parking garage and the human resources department. A sprinkle of rain caused traffic to slow down, but it wasn't enough to keep us from getting to Wendy's desk in record time. I couldn't have gotten there any faster if I'd been running late for work.

We were in and out in less than five minutes.

I couldn't remember the last time I'd mailed or received a genuine, handwritten letter. Christmas cards didn't count.

Katie stayed on my heels the whole way to her car. I finally ripped open the envelope and pulled out the neatly folded piece of cream-colored paper.

Rowan,

I hope this is you, anyway. I have been searching high and low, around the clock for you. Thanks to Google, one random article on a hospital website, and sorting through and eliminating over two hundred people whose first names start with the letter 'R' (long story), I hope I've finally found the real you. If this is you, and you're the Rowan Honeycutt from the Las Vegas marathon, I can't thank you enough for saving my life. You have restored my faith in humanity, and I'd love nothing more than to talk to you, or better yet thank you in person. My contact info is on my business card. And if this isn't you, then this is all really awkward, and my search will continue.

All my best,
Wesley Miller

P.S. If I don't hear back from you, I completely understand.

Holy shit. Wesley Miller? It was really him. *He found me*?

I stood in the middle of the hospital parking garage clinging to the letter, physically shaking and fighting back tears.

Kat snatched it out of my hands and skimmed over it.

"Oh my God, Rowan...it's..." She looked up at me, and we locked eyes. "It's freaking him! How did he find you? You have to call him. Where is his card?"

"I-I don't know, Kat. I don't even remember seeing it". I peeked inside the envelope, and there it was, as promised. Wesley's business card. I pulled it out and handed it to her without looking at it.

When did this become my life? Never in a million and twenty years did I think I would be on the receiving end of this kind of shit. I'd seen TV shows, watched movies and read books about people having these bizarre experiences and meetings, but not me, not in my lifetime.

We loaded ourselves into her car and she passed me the folded letter tucked neatly back into the envelope. "Rowan. You have to call him. I don't know anyone on the planet who would go through so much trouble to find someone, regardless of the circumstances. This is insane."

Kat was right. I shifted in the driver's seat to face her because I needed her to hear me out. "Look, I get it. But it's not just about how much trouble he went through to find me, which was a lot, I'm sure. I just don't have any good reason to contact him. He'll eventually get over having his life saved and move on. They always do. You know this." And the truth was, I was scared to death of getting any closer to him than I already had.

"If you say so." She looked at me like I'd completely lost my mind, because what she still didn't know, since I had yet to tell her, was Wesley and I had already met.

I lost count of how many times in a few short hours I looked at the envelope, scanned over every square inch of the letter, held it to my nose, appreciating its aroma because it smelled just like him—Wesley wore a scent no one would ever forget. And the only thing standing between me and this insanely gorgeous man were my own insecurities, one phone call or text, and over five hundred miles…because the envelope was postmarked Chicago, Illinois.

"Let me read it again," Chloe said, holding her hand out.

After Kat and I left the hospital, she dropped me off at home to go spend the rest of the afternoon with her boyfriend, Justin. Chloe stopped by not long afterward with a six-pack of beer and an ungodly number of shopping bags to show off her latest mall finds—all scattered and stacked across my dining room table and hung across the backs of the chairs.

I reluctantly gave her the envelope, worried that the more hands touched it, the more it would lose its scent.

She pulled out the contents and looked at his business card. "Wesley A. Miller, MD," she read out loud. "Impressive. And he's in emergency medicine? Come on, Rowe. This isn't a coincidence."

"We established all that, Chloe. What's your point?" I headed to the kitchen and started rummaging through my cabinets and fridge trying to compile a grocery list. Anything to get my mind off everything.

"Nothing, I guess. Just reminding you. In case you needed any more reason to call him."

There were a million reasons why I should call him, like, *Hey, thanks for catching me in your arms because I walk like a newborn baby calf in heels when I'm drunk.* Or, *You smell ungodly amazing, what scent is that, anyway? I might buy it for my next boyfriend.* Or, how about, *You're welcome for me saving your life, and I'd really like to sleep with you at some point, but I am, in a nutshell, a t-total train wreck.*

"Yeah, right. I don't need any more reason to call him." I poured myself a glass of wine and stared at the empty shelves. Screw the list. When I turned to head back to the dining room, Chloe had a big-ass grin on her face and my phone in her hand. "Chloe. What are you doing?

And why are you smiling like that?" I ran across the room and dove at her almost spilling my wine. "Did you just call him?"

She laughed and held my phone in the air like a game of keep-away. "Someone needs to because you're too chickenshit."

I launched at her, practically taking both of us to the ground, and snatched my phone from her hand. The screen was off. "I swear to God, I would have killed you if you called him." I stuck my phone in my back pocket, far out of her reach. All I needed was for him to call back an unknown number from a missed call, because I did not have enough self-control to not answer it.

I plopped down next to her, feeling a little more relaxed knowing she was just getting her rocks off toying with me. My phone vibrated with a text alert. When I looked at the screen, I almost passed out. The sneaky ho didn't call him—she'd sent him a text message.

TEN
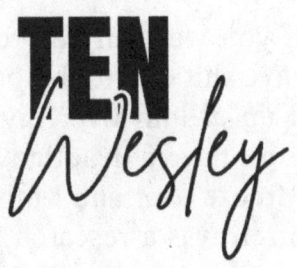

Wesley

"Having any luck?" Warren asked, taking a sip of his evening scotch. That was one good thing about my baby brother, he might have been dense, but we genuinely loved and cared about each other, and he always had my back. He'd been instrumental in helping me with my search for Rowan. I gave him half the list and he went to work on it. It was like she lived in the Federal Reserve. So far as I could tell, she had no Facebook, no Twitter, and no Instagram.

That was the glory of the internet. I could type in "Rowan" plus a last name from the registration list with the city and state for each name and hit *Search*. I was able to eliminate almost half the list based on images alone. The ones who didn't pop up on some form of social media platform, business website, or weren't listed on an obituary, got a handwritten letter to any physical address I could link to a name. The one good thing that worked in my favor was Rowan wasn't a very popular name.

I sighed. "Not yet. I've made it through more than half the names and mailed off few letters. Already hit a couple official dead ends from those who were nice enough to call me. I'm still waiting for a few more responses."

"Well, if you want any more of my help, let me know. I don't have shit else to do tonight."

I looked up at him over my laptop. "You? The workaholic doesn't have a deadline or research article to write? Did hell freeze over and I missed it?" I joked, but it was true. Warren was a research geek and had a love affair with his work.

"No, hell did not freeze over. I just didn't bring home any work tonight, asshole."

"Well, good for you. Maybe you're on the right track to not being forever single."

He flipped me off. "You're one to talk, dick. I'll have you know I've been out a few times with Daniel as of late."

"You?" I asked, with a raised eyebrow. "Since when did you stop working long enough to become his wingman?"

He outstretched his arms in the air. "I'm broadening my horizons."

"Whatever you need to tell yourself, but the only thing you're going to broaden by diving into his world is your STD spectrum. I mean that in the most lovingly way possible, of course."

"He lives an interesting life, for sure."

"Speaking of his lifestyle, did he tell you about his one-nighter in Vegas?"

He took another sip of his drink. "About four times, which seems like a lot of bragging, even for him."

"Yeah, she must have been one for the books if he's still talking about her. He told me she was a 'one and done.'"

Warren stood and stretched. "Well, whatever she was, she had nice tits; I'll give him that."

"You saw her?" I leaned back with my laptop in my lap and kicked my feet up on Warren's coffee table.

"She let him snap a few pics of her boobs."

"And he just randomly showed them to you?"

"Of course not," he said. "I asked to see. I need a refill. Want one?"

My glass was still just as full as it was when he poured it. Ever since I got sick a few years back, I'd been completely dry. He knew, but he offered one every time we were together. Besides, I wasn't about to risk getting *that* sick, ever again.

I held up my glass and showed it to him. "Nah, man, I'm good. Thanks."

He walked out of the room and my phone dinged with a new text message. *Fucking great.* I didn't even need to look at it to know who it was. It was the same person, trying to get a response out of me, and I was not in the mood for her games.

Warren came back with a freshly refilled glass of scotch. That amber liquid looked delicious, too. He had no idea how badly I wanted to snatch that cup out of his grip and slam it back. I couldn't even remember the last alcoholic drink I'd had.

"So, what's the game plan now? You have any plans for the night?"

I put my focus back on the screen in front of me and kept searching. Mostly I was double backing on my original search, going over all of the names, waiting…again. "Go cook dinner. I'm starving. You?"

"Finish this drink, take a shower, maybe jerk off."

"Sounds like you have an exciting evening planned out." My phone dinged again. "Fuck," I mumbled, out loud, more to myself than anything.

"Problems?"

"Something like that. It's Ashley. She won't leave me the fuck alone. She's been pestering me to talk since Vegas, but she never says what it is she wants to talk about, just that it *has* to be in person. Not in text or over the phone."

Warren let out a laugh. Asshole. "Sounds important. You should go meet up with her then, see what she wants."

"Real fucking funny. I'm glad you find my life so entertaining."

"Oh, don't flatter yourself. It's only mildly entertaining at best. Maybe she's pregnant again and wants to invite you to the baby shower. Wouldn't that be some shit?"

It didn't matter what she had to tell me; I'd already washed my hands of that train wreck a long time ago. "Good for her, then. Better that poor bastard than me." I shut down and packed up my laptop. "I'm going home to eat. Have fun jerking off."

We said our brotherly good-bye's and as I rode the elevator up two floors to my condo, because, yes, we lived in the same building, I checked my phone. I had two new text messages, neither of them from Ashley, surprisingly. But both were from numbers I didn't know. The first one just said wrong number. *I didn't message you, but fine.* The second one was from a 901-area code. *Got your letter. Will be in touch – Rowan Honeycutt.*

I almost dropped my phone as I stepped inside the foyer of my penthouse. *Rowan Honeycutt.* She was the one I'd found on the hospital website. For whatever reason, I knew deep down that this was her, that she was the one at the center of all of this. It took every ounce of energy I had to fight off the urge to call her number. Instead, I just typed out the response *Great. Can't wait.* The lamest text message I'd ever sent to anyone.

ELEVEN
Rowan

She'd actually done it. That ho sent him a text from my phone, and now, he had my number.

I spent the rest of the afternoon threatening to kick Chloe's ass for texting Wesley. She finally accepted defeat and I helped her load up her car with her new wardrobe and sent her home. Once she was gone, I reread his letter and the two-line text exchange.

After locking up my house and downing my second glass of wine, I took a shower and climbed into bed. A deep ache and need for release rolled through me in waves as I thought about that sexy man and his bright smile. The warmth and hardness of his body against mine.

My hands moved over my body, but I felt Wesley. I felt his warm hands skimming across my collarbone, massaging my breast, tracing down my stomach, touching me lower and lower, until finally he was where I wanted, where I *needed* him. As soon as I slid my fingers inside, I was lost to the thought of feeling him inside me. I arched off the bed, saying his name out loud as I let go of all the tension that had been building.

After cleaning up and pulling myself together, I climbed back into bed. I rolled onto my side, faced Wesley's letter on the pillow next to me, and stared at his phone number. Maybe it was the wine or the euphoria I felt from a much-needed orgasm, but against my better judgment, I called him.

It rang once, twice, three times. Shit, it was almost midnight.

Hang up already, Rowan. Hang. Up.

"Helllllo?" he answered with a deep, sleepy voice.

Oh hell.

He sounded so sexy and exactly how I remembered. I wondered if he slept naked. *Idiot!* He might not even be alone. *Did you ever consider that?* I asked myself. *No!* I slapped my forehead.

"Rowan? Is that you?" His voice vibrated through the speaker.

Oh God, oh God, oh God. What was I doing? I clearly woke him up in the middle of the night and had no freaking clue why I called or what to say. So, I did what any self-respecting woman would do when calling someone she didn't really know in the middle of the night. I hung up.

"Shit," I yelled out loud. "Shit, shit, shit. You friggin' moron." I slammed my phone down on the bed, and buried my face into my pillow, letting out a frustrated scream. As I regained control of my breathing, my phone rang.

Without even looking, I answered it. "How'd you know it was me?"

"Well, hi there." He let out a soft laugh. "Well, you texted me from this number earlier, and I don't know anyone else in Memphis, Tennessee or by the name of Rowan. But thanks for calling? I think?" He was probably wondering what the hell would possess me to randomly call him in the middle of the night.

"Sorry. I'm so sorry. I just—" Just what? *Think, Rowan, think.* "I got your letter and I wanted to thank you—well, let you know I read your letter. Obviously. Thank you for writing it. And yes, it's me. Rowan from Vegas. Actually, I'm from Memphis, but I was in Vegas." He was going to hang up on me. Good. Maybe that's what I needed, because clearly, I didn't know what in the hell I was doing. And I was still out of breath from the orgasm *he'd* recently given me. I must have sounded like a blubbering idiot.

His breathing, on the other hand, was slow and controlled. "Rowan," he finally said. "First off, calm down. It's just me. But I can't believe it's you. *The* Rowan Honeycutt, from Las Vegas and Memphis. And I'm the one who's supposed to be thanking you. You saved my life. So, thank you." He sounded so genuine and sincere, even if it was almost 1:00 a.m. "And second, don't ever be sorry for calling me. You can do it any time."

Every single word that came out of his mouth made me smile. By the time he finished talking, I finally had my nerves under control. "Well, you're very welcome. I'm glad I was there to help you."

"Me too. But let me tell you, finding you was no easy feat."

"Really?" I found that little tidbit of information mildly entertaining seeing as I hadn't done anything to hide myself.

He laughed softly. "Oh, you have no idea."

"Do tell. I'd love to hear all about it." As much as I wanted to know exactly how he found me, I really just wanted him to keep talking so I could listen to his voice.

I laid there in the dark with my phone pressed to my ear as he told me his side of the story.

"Wow, Wesley, that's a lot of work. But can I just say, I'm even more impressed you actually remember me."

"Of course. How could I ever forget someone like you? I remember a lot about you—the smell of your perfume mixed with your shampoo, the way your body felt molded against mine, how you physically relaxed in my arms when I spoke into your ear, like my words made you melt—yes, I remember. And knowing that I've found you, let's just say, that makes me one incredibly happy man."

Nothing was going to convince me that any of this was real—that he was real, and we were having this conversation. Because if we were, I was totally screwed. Done for. Finito.

"So, I'm curious," he said, with a slight hint of amusement. "Exactly how did *you* find *me*? In the hospital, I mean. I never gave you my name, and I was in the ICU. They don't let just anyone in there."

I practically choked on my own spit remembering what I had to do to get into the ICU since they only allowed family. But I cleared my throat and swallowed my pride. It was time to be a big girl. "Well, I... One of the medics who helped you—Evan was his name. I gave him my name and number at the race and told him to call me with an update, and he did." I answered in one long breath, hoping he wouldn't push to find out more.

"Evan? Huh, I don't remember anyone named Evan, but I do recall a Rowan *Miller* on a visitor pass? Does that name ring a bell?"

Ohmigod. Our conversation took a sharp, mortifying turn. "Wait, my visitor pass? You have my badge from the hospital? How did you get that?"

"Minor details."

Minor details my ass. He'd set me up and was enjoying every minute of it. I could practically hear him smiling when he spoke. Fine. Two could play that game. I sat straight up and squared my shoulders, just like my mother always said I needed to do or I'd end up hunchbacked. "Okay, you caught me," I told him with confidence. "I saved your life—the least you could have done was let me use your last name, pretending to be your wife, so I could visit you in the hospital." Boy, that sounded even more ridiculous saying it out loud than it did when I'd done it.

He laughed at my admission. "Very clever, Rowan Honeycutt. Though, I think I like Miller better. It has a nice ring to it."

Okay, so maybe he was the crazy one. But he wasn't wrong—I did kind of like the sound of Rowan *Miller*.

He gave me more hell about using his last name; I gave him hell for almost dying just to learn my first name. The coincidences and commonalities we shared were like something out of the *Twilight Zone*.

The conversation flowed a lot easier once everything was out in the open and I wasn't near as crazy as I might have initially come across to him, and he convinced me that he wasn't a stalker. With a promise to keep in touch, we finally hung up the phone a little after three in the morning because he had to be at work in a few hours.

Little by little, piece by piece, throughout that phone call, Wesley broke down tiny bits of the ironclad wall I'd carefully and meticulously crafted around my broken heart.

♡♡♡

The morning sun beamed between my bedroom curtains at what felt like was way too soon. "Uh, God. I have got to drink more water." I checked the time on my phone. It was almost ten in the morning. Katie was at work and had already texted me a handful of times.

Katie: Chloe said you sent Wesley a text? Really? You didn't tell me!!!
Katie: Helllloooo!?

102

If I didn't reply to Kat, I had no doubt she'd leave work and break down my door. I told her I just woke up and confirmed that it was Chloe who texted him, not me. Also that I spent half the night on the phone with him. Maybe she'd get off my ass about setting me up if she thought I had an interest in someone.

We agreed to some girl time after she got off work. She still worked as a respiratory therapist in the emergency room where I'd started as a nurse way too many years ago. A part of me missed all the action and working with her, but I was grateful for my time away from the bedside.

I shot Chloe a quick text inviting her back over for some more girl time with Kat. She declined my invite in favor of another date with Tanner.

A new text notification popped up from Wesley. My hands instantly started to shake. Then I realized he'd already sent me a few other messages before I'd ever even thought twice about crawling out of bed.

Wesley: Good morning, angel. Thanks for the great conversation, even if it cost me beauty sleep.

Wesley: I am really sorry. That was a little much.

Angel? His terms of endearment were not lost on me. It'd been so long since a man had called me by any kind of pet name, I'd forgotten what it felt like. I thought back on our late-night conversation and smacked myself on the forehead. I could not believe some of the things we had talked about, and he was worried about saying too much now?

Me: Good morning, Dr. Miller. It's going to take more than just a few text messages and sweet names to scare me off. I enjoyed our talk, too. Sorry I cost you your beauty sleep. I'm sure you're still beautiful. Forgive me?

Eventually, I made my way into the kitchen, popped a coffee pod into my Keurig, and waited for my coffee to brew. I didn't hear back from him for the rest of the day. He said he had to work, so I could only imagine how busy he was. That's life in the E.R—just another day in Paradise.

♡♡♡

Kat unlocked the front door just after eight later that night and strolled in like she owned the place.

"Come on in. Make yourself at home," I said to her with a whole lot of love and sarcasm.

She swiped the box of pizza off the kitchen counter and made her way to the living room, dropping herself on my couch. "Don't mind if I do."

"One of these days you might walk in and see something you're not ready to see."

"Oh, please, Rowe. It's not like I'm going to be walking in on some intimate moment. Plus, I have a key."

I grabbed the pizza from her and set it on the coffee table in front of us. "For all you know, I could have been going to town with my vibrator," I countered as I took a huge bite of my slice of supreme pizza.

"True, but very unlikely. That thing probably doesn't even have batteries, and if it does, I'm sure they're corroded."

Wrong. It didn't have any batteries. "Clearly, my sex life is way too predictable."

"That's unfortunate. Let's change that."

Oh, little did she know, I was already planning on it. "You're treading dangerous waters there, my friend." I had a feeling we were going in two different directions with matters of my sex life.

She smiled. "I live for danger."

"Spill it, Katie." She was plotting something. I'd inadvertently agreed to dipping my toes in the dating pool once we got home from Vegas, and she already had a line forming for me.

"Nope. I'm not saying a word," she said with a mouthful of pizza. "I wanna hear all about Wesley, first. Give me all the details from start to finish. Don't leave anything out."

Thank God. I was not ready for her to convince me why she needed to set me up with someone. Instead, I ran back over everything with her from the time Chloe got her claws on my phone, up until we talked on the phone, giving her a recap of most of our conversation. Some of the more *intimate* things we talked about I kept to myself.

"Wait a minute," she said, stopping me from telling her anymore. "You just said he told you he even remembered you from the hospital and the night before?

What about the night before? Friday? We were at karaoke."

"I did? You must've misunderstood me." Crap. I'd outed myself before I was ready.

"Nope. I'm pretty sure you just said he remembered you from the club *and* the race. Spill it. All of it."

This was the longest I'd ever kept anything from Katie since we'd been friends. I took a deep breath. "Okay, there's more." Then I admitted everything from how I'd crashed into him at the club and how he'd found me at the starting line of the race, what he remembered from the hospital, everything he went through to find me, and finally to Chloe texting him from my phone—which, as it turned out, I was super grateful for.

She sat there completely stunned.

"Well?" I said. "Say something, damn it. Don't just stare at me."

"You...I...Wait, what? First of all, you mean to tell me you ran full force, head to toe, with some hottie at the club, and didn't even bother to tell me? Then you saw him *again* out of tens of thousands of people at a marathon, and by some weird coincidence you also saved his life?" She sounded just as confused about it as I'd been. "Then to top it all off, you kept it from me?"

Oops. "I'm so sorry. I can't believe it either, Kat." It felt so good to finally talk to her about Wesley so openly. Not that I wanted to hide anything from her because she was my best friend.

"I am so happy for you, Rowan." She pulled me into a quick, tight hug. "I really hope all this turns into something. If not, at least it's a step in the right direction. Just don't ever, and I mean ever, keep shit like that from me again."

"I won't. Promise."

"So, no date with Chad, then?"

"Chad? That's the guy you've been chomping at the bit to set me up with?"

"Yes! He's a great guy, but I'll back off, unless you wanna just go grab a coffee or something with him."

Did I? I mean, I hadn't been on a first date since I met David. That was a long time to go between first dates. Then the thought of getting caught up with Wesley terrified me. *Everything* about him terrified me. I sighed. "We'll see. I kind of just want to start slow."

"You know where to find me if things don't work out." She got up and went to the kitchen to get a drink and I snuck in a peek at my phone.

Wesley: Finally home. What a day. Can you talk?

Kat was back before I had a chance to respond to him. She raised an eyebrow as she handed me a beer. "You have a look. What the hell did you do while I was gone a whopping thirty-four and a half half seconds?" I shoved my phone under my thigh, but it didn't go unnoticed. "You were texting him! Weren't you?"

Busted. "Ugh, okay, yes. I mean, no. I didn't text him…he texted me, but I didn't respond. He just got home from work."

"Well, don't let me stop you! Text the man back. Hell, call him for all I care. Just *do* something."

107

If only it were that easy. It'd been a long time since I'd had those kinds of conversations—the ones that made you giggle for no apparent reason and feel all warm and fuzzy inside. I had no clue what the fuck I was doing. It was bad enough Wesley had to put up with me over the phone. I didn't want Kat to bear witness to the debacle too.

"I'll wait," I said as if it was no big deal. "Maybe call him later. He's in Chicago, so we're in the same time zone."

She practically spit out her drink. "Chicago? Holy shit! So, he's really in Chicago? Like, for real, for real? That is *so* far away from here. I was hoping the postage was wrong or maybe he'd mailed the letter while on a business trip or something."

"Yeah, no such luck," I said. "Thanks for the reminder. He's most definitely in Chicago." That was just the hard reality of it.

We sat on the couch, ate pizza, drank beer, and watched HGTV. After two episodes of *My Lottery Dream Home*, Kat stood and stretched. "As much as I hate to do this, I gotta get home. It's late and I need out of these nasty scrubs and a shower."

I hugged her again. "Thank you, Kat."

She pulled back and held me at arm's length. "Always. Everything is going to be okay. Now, go call him." That was all she said as she headed for the door.

I locked up behind her, turned off the kitchen light, and stood there leaning against the door in the dark trying to make heads or tails of my life, when my phone lit up on the couch across the room.

Lyndsay Marie

My heart fluttered.

TWELVE
Rowan

I ran across my house and dove for my phone.

It was my mom. *Damn.* "Hey, Mom," I answered.

"Rowan! It's your mother."

"Yes, I know who you are."

"How are you?"

"I'm fine. I'm guessing y'all are home now? How was your trip?"

"Yes, we're home. Just made it in last night. It was just wonderful, Rowan. I'm not interrupting anything, am I?"

"Nope, not at all. Kat just left."

"How is she? I haven't seen Katie in ages."

"She's really good. Just working a lot. Sounds like y'all had fun."

"Oh, we did. We only saw half of what we wanted to. We're planning to go back in a few weeks. You'll have to go one day. So, tell me about your trip. How was the race?" I didn't know how to answer that. So much had changed since the last time we talked. There were times in a girl's life when all she wanted to do was call her mom and tell her all the things, important or not, like how I saved a man's life in the middle of a road and now I was freaking crazy about him. But instead of dishing out all of the details about Vegas, I sugar-coated over the race and skipped anything that involved Wesley—which was most of my trip. So, there ended up not being much to say.

"Well, it sounds like you girls had a good time. So, listen. We're all getting together at your Grandma Lily's for dinner soon. I know the family would love to see you," she said in a tone that almost made it sound like it was my fault we didn't see each other more often.

I hadn't been to a large family gathering since, well, I couldn't remember when. Figured now was just as good of a time as any to start going to those again. "That sounds nice. Let me know when."

"Wonderful! I'm so excited. I'll call your grandmother in the morning and tell her to expect you there. She is going to be thrilled."

"She sure is, Mom. Caaan't wait."

"Well, I need to get off here and get ready to go to bed. We love you, Rowan. We'll talk soon."

"Okay, Mom, love you too." I disconnected the call. No sense in dragging it out and making the conversation any more awkward than it already felt.

I laid on the couch in total darkness, welcoming the silence. My phone was still in my hand, taunting me to call Wesley. I wanted to hold off for the sake of not coming across as some desperate and lonely woman who just couldn't resist him.

But I caved.

He answered on the second ring. "Well, good evening, Miss Honeycutt." His voice was warm, like whiskey. I was toast.

There was no way he was real. No man sounded *that* sexy and had the looks to match. It was one or the other, but not both.

I smiled so big my cheeks burned. "Good evening to you, Doctor," I said, trying to match his level of sexiness without being too obvious. "Sorry it's so late, but Katie stopped by after work, then my mom called."

"It's no problem. I'm just glad you called."

"So, how was your day?" I wanted to know every detail about his day from the time he woke up until now. And if I had my way, I'd be the last person he talked to before he went to bed because I'd established that he was, in fact, single and alone in bed the night I drunk called him.

He yawned into the phone. "Things are kind of slow right now. Nothing too exciting or intense. What about you? How was yours?"

"Hmm, it was okay, I guess. I cleaned up, helped my neighbor do some yard work, did laundry. Same ole, same ole." There really wasn't much to do when you lived alone, were primarily unemployed, and it was almost the middle of winter.

He let out a small laugh. "That sounds…exciting. Okay, no, it doesn't, but I'd much rather have been there with you doing all of that than be here."

Really? Did he mean that? He must have meant it, or he wouldn't have even said it. *Right?* I took his words to heart and ran with it anyway. "You know what? Me too, actually. Having you here would have made my day a hell of a lot more interesting."

"Well, we need to make it happen."

He'd caught me completely off guard. "Wait, what? Are you being serious?"

"Of course I'm serious," he said. "First off, I would never have suggested it if I didn't want to. Two, I work like eight days a month. Sometimes ten. I have all the time in the world. And third, Rowan, I have done nothing but think about you, since the first time I laid my eyes on you. You're all I've thought about from the time I wake up until the time I close my eyes at night. I want to see you as the clumsy and ridiculously beautiful woman who fell into my arms, not just someone who saved my life."

I was rendered absolutely speechless. I wanted all of that too, so much, but how was I supposed to tell him that without sounding despondent? "Wesley, I don't...I don't know what to say. I mean, yes, I want to see you too. But how? It's not like we live across town from each other." I had so much hope that he—*we*—could somehow make this happen. It's five hundred and thirty-two miles to Chicago from Memphis. Not that I looked. Okay, I totally looked.

"Minor details. Let me worry about them. Just say yes."

I held my breath. This was it. It was now or never. When I finally breathed, the word "yes" came out.

"Perfect," he said. Then his tone shifted from playful to something dark and daring. "But just to prepare you, Rowan, I don't think I'm going to be able to keep

114

my hands off of you once I get you in my arms." His words came out like a warning. A hot, sexy warning, and I was going to fall right into his trap.

"Good," I said, "because I feel the same way about you, Wesley Miller. I've wanted nothing more than to be reminded of what it feels like having your arms wrapped around me."

"Have you thought about how my hands would feel caressing your bare skin? Because I have."

I swallowed hard. He went there. "Actually, I have." *Every day and night.*

"What else have you thought about, Rowan?"

That was a loaded question. "Do you really want to know that?"

"I want to know everything," he said. "Because you have been the main attraction in all of my thoughts."

Without thinking twice, I slid my hand beneath the waistband of my shorts, deep down into the slick wetness between my legs. I closed my eyes, and there he was again—it was his hand sliding up and down; his fingers moving in and out; his palm against my clit.

A soft moan escaped my lips.

"Rowan," he let out a soft groan. "Are you touching yourself?"

"Mmm. Maybe."

"Imagine that's my hand—those are my fingers sliding deep inside that sweet pussy of yours."

My fingers slid deeper inside. "Hmmm."

"That's it, baby. Keep going, but do not come."

"Wes…Wesley. Ah, I need to." I could hear his hand pumping up and down as he gripped his cock, anticipating his own release. My breathing quickened as my hand moved faster and faster. He let out a deep groan into the phone. I envisioned him pumping faster and faster until he said the words "Rowan. Come for me. Now. I'm, I'm com—fuck."

...

"I still cannot believe your life, right now, Rowan. This is stuff for the books," Kat said, burying her nose in a fluffy pink rose as she walked past my dresser.

I'd given Wesley my home address so he could send me a thank-you card. He made it crystal clear he was not thanking me for the phone sex we'd been having almost every time we talked, but for everything else. It'd apparently slipped his mind that not only was he going to send more than one card, but each and every one would be attached to a massive bouquet of flowers. He also forgot to mention that I'd receive a new one every day.

"Me either," I said. "I don't know what I did to deserve him, but he is ridiculously amazing." We talked and exchanged texts every single day and night, around the clock since I'd taken that leap and called him. Our conversations grew longer and longer each time we talked, and our text messages became sweeter and sexier and definitely dirtier.

"And you haven't even slept with him yet," Chloe said deadpan.

"Not everyone sleeps with someone to get flowers, Chloe," Kat tossed back, jokingly.

116

Chloe rolled her eyes. "That was one time. Look, all I'm saying is after all this—" She waved her hand at the bouquets of flowers that took up the entire top of my dresser. "—is she better fuck his brains out if he does show up."

Oh, he was showing up. I had no doubt about it. I half expected to see him by now, just because he apparently liked surprises, but he said he'd let me know when he was coming because he didn't want to intrude on my life. He just needed to work out a few things at home, first. If he only knew how much I wanted him to storm his ass up in here unannounced. My nerves were shot just thinking about it.

"Thanks, again, y'all for helping me out today." I'd finally made the decision to replace the one constant reminder of mine and David's relationship—our mattress.

Kat wiped the sweat off her forehead with the back of her arm and cracked open the bedroom window to let in some crisp winter air. "You're welcome," she said. "And I don't care who fucks who, but if you ever decide to buy a new mattress, or any piece of furniture for that matter, please call a professional mover." She flopped backward onto the middle of my brand-new bed.

Me and Chloe joined her. "You guys are the professionals," I said to her knowing damn well we had no business hauling away my old king-sized mattress and replacing it with a new one by ourselves. "I still love y'all though."

"We love you too," they said at the same time.

117

Once they'd finally left, I shut and locked my bedroom window, made up my brand new bed in fresh, clean linens that smelled like springtime, and then jumped in the shower to wash off the grime from the day.

At one point, I felt brief pang of guilt when we were struggling to haul out my old mattress to Kat's dad's truck. After all, that was the bed where David and I had spent a third of our relationship either sleeping or other things…but I knew deep down I couldn't bring another man into that bed. It just didn't feel right.

After I showered, I threw on a pair of cotton shorts and a tank top and crawled into bed. All I needed was to get Wesley here.

My phone vibrated, and my body tingled from head to toe at the sight of Wesley's name lighting up the screen.

Wesley: I hope you're still enjoying the flowers. You should be getting one more package today.

Seriously?

Me: You are too much, Dr. Miller.

Wesley: Only for you.

My bed was just getting warmed up when the doorbell rang. I debated on even getting up to see who it was, but Wesley said he'd sent me something else. At the risk of whatever it was freezing on the porch, I reluctantly threw back the covers and climbed out of bed. The last

118

few bouquets he'd sent were delivered in ding-ding-ditch style. So, answering the door wearing practically nothing was the least of my concerns.

Except, when I opened my front door, I was suspended in place at the site in front of me.

Time froze like the ground outside.

THIRTEEN

Rowan

I scanned the silhouette in front of me and staring back were those dark and mysterious hazel-brown eyes I'd been so desperately wanting to see, and not just in pictures and videos on my phone. Wesley's tall, tan, and very masculine outline filled the doorway, towering over me.

I blinked in disbelief. "You're here? Are you really here?"

He smiled and dimples appeared. "I am," he said. "And these—" He held out another gigantic bouquet of white roses. "—are for you."

I stepped forward to meet him in the doorway. When I put my hand on his clean-shaven face, he closed his eyes and pressed his cheek into my hand.

"Wesley, I've needed to see you again. So much."

He stepped under threshold, closing the space between us. "You have no idea just how desperate I've been for this very moment right here, right now." He set his carry-on bag down just inside the door.

Our eyes locked and we exchanged a million words without saying a thing.

The bouquet of flowers dropped from his hands to the floor. He held out his arms, and without hesitation, I jumped into him and wrapped my legs around him.

"Ah. Careful," he said. "Chest is still a little sore."

"I'm so sorry. I'll get down."

"The hell you will." He tightened his grip around my waist.

There was a time in my life, not too long ago, I would have done everything in my power to avoid anything that had to do with a man. But I held on to him like my life depended on it.

I couldn't take it anymore. My mouth found his. His soft, full lips welcomed mine No more waiting, no small talk, no teasing. Just two people with an intense and passionate need for each other.

We held our mouths locked together as he kicked the door shut behind him. "Bedroom," he demanded in a low growl into my mouth. "Now. Please."

I pointed behind me. "Just walk." And he did, kissing me the entire time. Eventually, I pulled back for air and trailed kisses across his jaw and down to his neck. His pulse thrummed beneath my lips. He was real and every part of him tasted like heaven. I licked from the base of his throat back up to his ear, pulling his earlobe between my teeth.

"Fuck," he hissed through his teeth. "I swear to God I'm going to come in my pants if you keep doing that. It has been a very, very long time, Rowan."

121

"We have all day. Feel free to do it more than once."

He peeled me off of his body and stood me on the floor in front of him. "You're right. We do have all day, and I intend on taking full advantage of every single second of it with you. I've wanted this moment since the first night I laid my eyes on you." He pulled the pins loose from my hair and tossed them to the floor. It felt like he'd pulled the pin from a grenade and I was about to explode. "I cannot wait," he said as he gave my hair a tug, loosening it, "to pull this from behind."

"Wesley," I whispered, my voice laced with desperation.

He bent down and softly kissed my lips, my neck, pulling my tank top strap to the side, kissing my shoulder. His hold on my hair tightened, pulling me back as he pushed forward, pinning me between him and the edge of my bed.

Oh! He wanted me to feel *him*. Every. Single. Inch. I buried my face into his chest and inhaled. He smelled exactly like I remembered. That alone was enough to make me completely lose my mind.

"Feel that?" He rolled his hips, pressing his erection into me. "That, babe, is all because of you and all for you." With his hands on my hips, he lifted me onto the bed. "I cannot tell you enough what it means to me to be here with you right now, but I am going to show you."

"I need you," was all I said. The next thing I knew we were in the middle of the bed, kissing so hard my lips burned.

122

He grabbed the hem of my shirt, pushing it up to my neck, exposing my bare chest. I'd never felt so vulnerable and comfortable at the same time.

"You're so fucking beautiful," he said right before he wrapped his mouth practically around my entire boob and sucked so hard, I cried out. He pulled back and looked up at me like he'd injured me.

"Sorry." I smiled. "It's been a while. You're good. Keep going."

He explored my chest, while his hand slid down my side to my thigh. I gathered my shirt and pulled it off. He stopped kissing me. I propped up on my elbows. "What's wrong?"

"Absolutely nothing. I just want to take a break and look at you before I completely lose my damn mind."

Oh, I'd already lost it all to him—my body, my mind, and my heart was well on its way. I was a goner.

He slid up close and kissed me gently on the lips. Not the rushed, frenzied kind. This one was slow and controlled. The weight of him on top of me and the feel of him pressing between my legs was too much.

"Wesley, I need you. Now," I said, trying not to lose contact with his mouth or any other part of him.

He braced himself on one arm, reached over his shoulder behind his back, and pulled his T-shirt off in one smooth movement. It was the sexiest thing I had ever witnessed a man do. And that was when I saw his scar.

"Hey," he said softly. "It's okay. I know what you're thinking. I'll be fine. We'll talk about it later. Okay?" He planted a soft kiss on my forehead. Then on my cheek, chin, neck, chest, and down to my stomach…then lower.

"Okay," I said focusing on him.

He trailed his tongue along the curve of my hip, pulling my shorts off as he went, making his way to the inside of my thigh. He spread my legs and gave me an agonizingly slow, deep lick from the back all the way to the front.

"Holy shit," I panted. I wanted to grab the back of his head and push his face between my legs. Instead, he got up and finished undressing himself.

For the first time in years, I was about to give myself completely to another man.

He climbed back on the bed, positioned himself directly over me, completely covering my entire body, like the fucking god that he was.

My heart raced so fast I could have blacked out. I wrapped my legs around his waist, giving him full access to all of me. He slowly pushed himself inside of me, sending us both in a downward spiral into pure ecstasy.

As soon as he was inside of me, he went still. "Give me a minute or I'm going to come."

I pulled him down and kissed him hard. He'd barely moved, and I was already there. "Fuck me, Wesley." I dug my heels into him as he picked up his pace.

"You are so tight and so wet, Rowan." Sweat dripped off his forehead onto my neck and chest.

"I'm. Going. To. Come. Now. Please…" My words came out each time he pushed deeper inside of me.

Then I moaned and screamed his name. He immediately followed my lead as my name roared from his lips.

"I'm not a smoker, but if I was, this would be the perfect time for one," he said as he kissed my forehead.

I laid beside him, tucked under his arm with my head on his chest, recovering from the most intense sex I'd ever had. "Now that is the truth. And for the record, I'm glad you don't smoke."

"Me too. But I promise you though," he said confidently, "rounds two, three, and four will last a hell of a lot longer than that. I don't ever remember busting a nut that fast in my life, even as a teenager."

That made me laugh. "Two, three, and four? Huh. You're pretty confident in that statement." I knew damn well we were going to have a few more rounds. Not because the first one was fast, but because we finally got what we'd been waiting for and it was perfect. At least I thought so, anyway. "I'm glad it was quick because that was intense, and I don't think I could have gone on for much longer like that."

He trailed his fingers lazily up and down my back. "You would if I tied you down."

"Um-hmm. So how long do I have you for? When do you go home?" If I had my way, I'd keep him forever.

He blew out a sigh. "Tomorrow afternoon. I booked the latest possible return flight that would still get me home with enough time to sleep before going back to work."

Shit. There went my plans to keep him here forever.

He yanked me on top of him in one fast move, our bodies still covered in sweat from our frenzied sexcapades. "You ever going to ask me about it?"

"About what?"

"You know what. My scar. I mean, it is the reason we're together, and you've been running your fingers all over me, except here," he said, pointing to the top of his scar.

I touched the spot where his finger had been. He was right. We both knew it was something we needed to talk about, eventually, but then I would have to accept that he was a sick man.

"Okay," I finally said, looking into his dark eyes. "Tell me. What happened?" I braced myself because I didn't want to think about losing, or almost losing, him again.

He took in a deep breath and told me about his past—his medical history, the surgeries, failed treatments, his first brush with death. I was terrified. I laid my head on his chest and listened to his voice and his heartbeat as he spoke.

"So," he finished, "when all other treatments failed, my last resort was a full transplant or death. My heart's good now, it's just these immunosuppressive drugs keep me at risk for getting sick. That's how we met. I caught some shit in Hawaii. Now here we are."

His story was out in the open now.

Images of David crept in the forefront of my mind. The night I lost him, the night I failed to save him, the night I'd worked so hard to forget. It was all too much. And the fact that David was an organ donor and died the same month Wesley had his transplant…I didn't even want to go there. I was sick of all of the coincidences, and did my best to block it out, like everything else I didn't want to accept.

Then, right on cue as his way of changing the subject, his dick twitched underneath me. I looked up at him, and he smiled the cheesiest shit-eating grin.

I smiled back and pushed myself up to straddle him, bracing myself on his shoulders. I slowly rocked my hips back and forth, rubbing against him. He was ready to go just that quick, and so was I. He dug his fingers into my hips and positioned himself to enter me.

"Sit," he commanded.

So I did. All the way down without hesitation. Every inch of him felt like heaven.

FORUTEEN
Rowan

We spent the rest of the day and night, and the entire next day literally between the sheets of my bed, breaking in the mattress from top to bottom.

It dawned on me as Wesley sat across the dining room table, sipping his coffee, going over his flight itinerary, David hadn't crossed my mind one time. There was no guilt for sleeping with another man or having another man in what was once *our* home. It was only me and Wesley nonstop the entire time.

"What's on your mind over there, sexy?"

I took a sip of coffee. "Just thinking about how amazing you are."

He raised an eyebrow. "You're pretty amazing yourself, beautiful. Anything else?"

"Yeah." I let out a sigh. "I have to attend a family get-together, and it's been a looong time since I've seen them. Just a little nervous about seeing everyone again."

He smiled and let out a soft laugh. "I hate to hear that, but if it makes you feel any better, I can relate. Me and my family aren't exactly close either. It's mostly just

128

me and my brother, Warren, now. Gatherings are kind of a bust for us too." He took a sip of his coffee, the steam rising up around his eyes. Who knew drinking coffee could be so sexy but leave it to Wesley Miller to do it.

"That's it? Just you two?"

"Yup. Me and Warren. Growing up there was five of us—me, Warren, Wyatt, in that order, and our mom and father, Van Buren. No extended family. We lost Wyatt to childhood cancer when he was six. Then a few years ago, our mom lost her battle with cancer." He paused. "Her death caused some tension, we'll call it, between me and Warren and our father because she left all of her inheritance from her dad, our grandfather, to me and Warren, totally bypassing Van Buren. That really pissed him off. Then some more bullshit drama went down last year with the three of us, and that was the final straw for me. I completely cut him off." He shrugged it off dismissively. "What can you do?"

"I'm really sorry about your mom and brother," I said. "I can't imagine."

"You learn to live…just differently. Finish telling me about your family."

"There's not much to say. My relationship with my mom is weird. She left my dad when I was twelve and he killed himself. Things haven't been the same since." Now was not the time to bring up David.

I decided to lighten up the mood a little. "Sounds like your mom and dad had a thing for the *W* names, didn't they?"

He laughed. "They did. And *A* middle names. Wesley Alan, Warren Abram, and Wyatt Alexander."

129

"Wow. That or she liked the initials *W.A.M.*"

"No kidding." He stood from the table and walked over to me, pulled me up from my chair, and held me in his arms. "I know you've lost a lot of people, but you have me now too. And I can promise you one thing, Rowan, I'm not going anywhere."

Deep down, I believed him. Who else would have gone through the lengths he had to find or see me? My own mother lived down the road, and I hadn't seen her in over a month.

I ran my hands through his hair, still damp from our morning shower, and traced my lips and teeth softly over the stubble on his jaw.

He let out a low growl. "You better watch yourself, babe, or I'll bend you over this table and make you come so fast you won't know what hit you."

I pressed up on my tiptoes and gave him a slow, soft kiss on the lips as I reached between us and rubbed my hand down his rock-hard length through his boxers. "Promise?"

If there was one thing I'd learned in that very moment about Wesley Alan Miller, when he made a promise, he kept it.

♡♡♡

"Thank you for the best time I've probably ever had. You really are something special."

"Thank you for having me," Wesley said as he held me in his arms. He gave me a long, deep kiss that sent chills from head to toe. It was one filled with promise, lust, and desire, the kind that you never wanted to end, and you wondered if you'd ever kiss that way again. "Don't worry, we'll see each other again soon."

Wesley had proven in a very short amount of time that he did exactly what he said he was going to do, and then some. "I can't wait," I said, trying to hide the disappointment in my voice knowing his Uber was on the way to take him to the airport. He'd insisted on getting his own ride so I wouldn't have to get out in the cold.

"I'm going to make one more quick sweep of your bedroom and make sure I didn't forget anything." He gave me another quick kiss, then disappeared to the back of the house.

I was in so deep with him already. I swiped my phone off the counter and tapped out a quick text to Katie and Chloe. They both needed to know I was still alive, since neither of them had heard from me since Wesley showed up and I sent them both a "Do not disturb - Wesley is here" text.

As I typed out my message, Wesley's phone buzzed against the granite countertop next to me. The screen lit up, and I fought the urge to look. *Fuck it*, I told myself. It was just a glance. It wasn't like I was picking it up and going through it. I looked down at his phone, and the name "Ashley Fletcher" was in the blue pop-up window, with the words "Call me when you get home. We need to talk," just below it.

I leaned back against the counter. Well, damn. That was the last thing I wanted to see right before he left me to go home to fucking Chicago. *Don't be ridiculous, Rowan. You barely know this guy...even though you just*

*spent the last twenty-four hours having unprotected sex
with him. Ugh, dumbass.*

Before I could do anything irrational, Wesley
rounded the corner. "Looks like I'm all set..." He
stopped directly in front of me. "What's wrong? You
look like you've seen a ghost."

"Nothing's wrong," I told him, trying my best to
hide my obvious sudden change in emotions. I never did
have a poker face. "I'm just not ready for you to leave.
That's all." Which was totally true, even still. But I would
have much rather had him here with me than in Chicago
with Ashley.

He picked up his phone, checked the screen, then
slid it in his front pocket. "Trust me. I don't want to leave
either, but my ride is almost here, and I have to work in
the morning." He grabbed my hand and led me toward
the front door. I held on tight, completely unsure of how
many more surprise visits he'd make, or if Ashley were
going to be an issue, or if I'd ever actually see him again.

A car pulled up and parked in the driveway. "I
think your Uber is here," I said, pointing out the living
room window.

He grabbed his bag off the floor. "I'll see you
soon, and you know I'll be in touch," he assured me as he
wrapped his hand around the back of my head, pulled me
toward him, and gave me one last kiss.

I opened the front door and watched him walk
away. Once he was in the car, I closed and locked the
door as they drove away.

My phone was still in my hand, and I realized I'd
never finished my text to Kat and Chloe.

Me: I am totally falling for him.

Instead of pressing Send, I deleted the message and typed out a new one.

Me: Girls night?

♡♡♡

"Glad you took off enough time from dating to finally come see me," I said to Chloe as she danced her way past me wearing a backpack, holding up a bottle of rum in one hand and her phone in the other, with "Welcome to the Jungle" blaring from its speaker. She'd clearly long gotten over the whole *my ex is dating your cousin* fiasco.

"Uh, ma'am, first, you're the one who's been locked away in your little sex dungeon. Second, I've been on at least three dates with the same guy."

I just shook my head and closed the front door. "Uh, ma'am," I said, mocking her tone. "It was literally twenty-four hours, and good for you."

"Whatever. Where's Kat?" she asked. "I figured she'd be here by now?"

"I talked to her about an hour ago. She said she'd be here in a bit." I wasn't the least bit worried about her. When she said she'd be somewhere, she meant it.

I followed behind Chloe as she danced her way into the kitchen where she dumped her stuff on the counter and pulled a bottle of wine out of her backpack. "Well, text her to hurry the fuck up. Tell her Captain

133

Morgan is waiting for her. Here," she said, handing me the wine. "This is for you since you don't usually drink the hard stuff."

I uncorked the bottle and poured myself a glass. "Thanks for looking out."

Chloe poured herself a shot of rum, then made a mixed drink of rum and Diet Coke. She knocked back the shot and chased it with her mixed drink. "So, what's new? Tell me about your binge sex with lover boy. You completely went off grid when he showed up. Thanks for the courtesy text."

I took another hefty sip of wine.

Just as I was about to start dishing out dirty details, the front door flew open. Chloe and I swung our heads in the direction of the living room. "What the hell?"

"Someone get me a drink. I know Chloe didn't show up empty-handed." Katie blew into the kitchen like a tornado, hair a complete mess, makeup smudged.

"Woah, slow down there Britney '07. What the hell happened to you?" I asked as Chloe filled two shot glasses.

Chloe handed Kat a glass. "Looks like Justin happened."

I rolled my eyes.

Katie grabbed one of the shots from Chloe, tossed it back, then slammed it down on the counter. "You'd be correct. Don't say a fucking word, neither of you. Just give me a refill."

Chloe handed her shot to Kat and she drank it up.

"Jesus, was it that bad?" Chloe asked, taking a sip of her mixed drink.

"No. That's the problem. It's never bad. We yell and fight, then the next thing I know we're going to town like teenagers." She sat down at the dining room table with a loud and dramatic huff. "Why? Y'all, why? Why can't I just let him go? We are so bad for each other, and the only time we are good together is in bed. Beyond that, we suck as a couple."

I'd agree with that, but I also didn't think neither Chloe nor I were in a position to offer relationship advice. We all knew Justin and Katie were bad for each other, but as much as we tried to convince her of it, she was not going to let him go until she was ready.

"Come on, let's go sit in the living room. I need to be comfortable if we're going to have this conversation," Chloe said, swiping the bottle of rum, tucking it under her arm. I grabbed my bottle of wine, and Kat begrudgingly got up and followed us.

We all plopped down on the couch. Chloe and Katie passed the bottle of Captain back and forth between them, Katie bitching about Justin each time she took a sip.

"Enough about me and my deranged love life. Tell us about your twenty-four-hour sex-fest with Wesley, or did you already dish it all to Chlo?"

Annnd we were back to me. Yay. "No, I haven't told her anything. You stormed in here like a crazed lunatic before I had a chance."

We sat there drinking, as I caught them up on as much as I could without going into too much detail, seeing as practically our entire time together was spent naked or screwing.

"Sounds like he's got it pretty bad for you. I mean, what other man would fly halfway across the country at the drop of a hat, show up unannounced, and screw you into oblivion?" Chloe asked.

"A crazed serial killer," Kat answered before I had a chance to respond. She had a point, but here I was, alive and well. Before I could defend her 'crazed serial killer' theory, she pulled her legs up and curled into a ball, snuggling into a throw blanket.

Chloe gave her a shove. "Oh no you don't. You better wake your ass up."

Too late. Katie was passed out and snoring like a grizzly bear. Good sex and a few shots of Captain Morgan will do that to a girl. "I'm not picking her up," Chloe said, as she stretched out and propped her feet up on the coffee table. "She's going to have to wake up right here on your couch."

No sooner did Chloe give Kat crap about falling asleep than she passed out.

Great. Then there was one.

FIFTEEN
Rowan

Family gatherings have always been one of my favorite pastimes. I loved everything about them—the food, the board games, uncontrollable laughing, dessert.

David's funeral was the last time I'd been around all of my family at once.

I parked at the curb of my Grandma Lily's Midtown bungalow a few minutes ahead of schedule. My mind flooded with a million childhood memories—all the holidays I'd celebrated at her house, the countless hours Grandma Lily and I spent decorating and cooking and how she'd let me stay up as late as I wanted to. Oh, to be four again.

Suddenly I felt an overwhelming guilt for not visiting her more often. Once every couple of weeks wasn't near enough.

I checked myself out in the rearview mirror one more time and gave up with a sigh. A sleek black Mercedes pulled up behind me. "Here we go."

As I reached for the door handle, a dark shadowy figure knocked on the driver's-side window, causing me to jump. "Shit." I opened the door and got out. "You scared me half to death, Aunt Lara. Don't you know this is Memphis and you can't just go knocking on peoples' windows."

"Oh, Rowan, don't be silly. I can't believe you're here! Anita said you were comin', but I didn't believe her."

"Yeah. I'm here. Believe it."

Jensen stood off to the side behind Lara, with a sour look on her face, picking at her fingernails. "Hey, Jensen," I said to her in my half-assed effort to be civil. If we had to spend the next few hours together, I wanted it to be as painless as possible.

She rolled her eyes and gave a small, lazy flick of her wrist without saying a word.

"Okay, guess I'll see y'all inside."

I walked up the driveway toward the house and heard my Aunt Lara call out behind me. "Jensen! Please come help me get all this stuff out of the car! Half of this is yours."

I looked over my shoulder and watched as Jensen kept walking towards the house. "You gonna help your mom or act like you didn't just hear her ask you for help?"

"Mind your fuckin' business, Rowan."

Well, okay then.

I ignored her, turned, and headed back to the car. I carried grocery bags stuffed with knew what, and a dish of food into the house. I was immediately greeted with the smells of culinary heaven wafting from the kitchen, followed by my mom and Grandma Lily, both with arms outstretched, trying to take things from me and hug at the same time.

"Oh, gosh, Rowan." My mom beamed as she took the casserole dish from my grip, simultaneously pulling me into her for a quick hug. "You look absolutely beautiful." Then she disappeared into the kitchen at the back of the house just as fast as she'd appeared. Exactly as I expected—short and to the point. Nothing more, nothing less.

Grandma Lily hobbled her four-foot-something frame over to me after greeting Aunt Lara and Jensen. I pulled her into the biggest, tightest hug.

When she let go, she looked me up and down. "You've grown," she said in only a way a grandmother could say to a woman in her thirties and get away with it.

I rolled my eyes. "Thanks, Grandma, but I think I stopped growing a long time ago, unless you're insinuating I've gained weight?" I gave her a suspicious look.

She flicked her false teeth around her mouth, reached behind me, and patted me on the ass but didn't say a word. I guess that settled it, which surprised me considering I was the lightest I'd ever been in my life. Then she disappeared into the kitchen where Mom and Lara were setting up the finishing touches on our late lunch / early dinner.

Great Uncle Bill, Grandma Lily's brother, sat on the couch watching the Hallmark Channel and stayed out of the way until it was time to eat. Poor guy was only one of two male presences left since Grandpa Franklin moved on to the big man in the sky. The only other man around now was my stepdad, Sam, who would rather take a toothpick through his eye than watch the Hallmark Channel with Bill, and Sam was nowhere to be seen.

"Hey, Uncle Bill," I called out to him as I made my way into the dining room.

"Hey, Rowan," he mumbled back. I gave him three minutes tops and he'd be dozing off for probably his second nap of the day.

As soon as I set everything down, Mom called out from the kitchen that it was time to eat. If there was one thing this family did right, it was food.

"That meal was perfect, y'all." I said a silent thank-you that I'd worn stretchy pants. If I hadn't actually grown yet, as Grandma Lily suggested, I sure as hell did after eating not one, but two plates of turkey, ham, mashed potatoes with gravy, corn bread, sweet potato casserole, collard greens, and cranberry sauce. My family, no matter how much we shrunk in numbers, would always cook enough food to feed an army. Grandma Lily expected us to eat it.

"We're all glad you made it out," Grandma Lily said. "We've missed you. You should come around more often. You know I can't drive anymore. I gotta rely on your mother or my neighbor, Patsy. And her vision ain't so good anymore."

I cringed at the thought of two women—one half-blind, one half-deaf—riding the streets of Memphis. "I know, Grandma, I will. I promise. Next time you need something, call me. I'll take you."

Growing up, our family had been close. We'd celebrated every holiday, major and minor, with her,

140

Grandpa Franklin, and a ton of extended family, right here in this house. Twenty years ago, this table held at least thirteen people shoved shoulder to shoulder, while the rest of us ate where we could find a place to sit or stand. Somewhere along the way, families broke up, people disbursed, and what we had left was sitting comfortably around an eight-person table.

"Wouldn't that be something? You'd be the first granddaughter to offer." She cut her eyes at Jensen, who was staring down at her phone. "But don't worry." She looked back at me. "I won't bother you. I can't get all the latest gossip in the senior community if I start hanging out with you."

I pushed back from the table, stood, and grabbed my empty plate. "It was delicious. Thank y'all again." I bent down and kissed my grandma's cheek. "Stay out of trouble." Then I walked to the kitchen.

I heard Grandma Lily ask everyone, "Who's ready for dessert?" I almost threw up thinking about it, but I never turned down one of her homemade desserts.

She shuffled into the kitchen and started milling around and handed me two dessert dishes. "Here, take these to the dining room."

"Yes, ma'am." I did as I was told and sat the dessert dishes down in an empty spot on the dining table. Lara and my mom each took turns going back and forth clearing the table of dirty dishes and replacing them with desserts and clean dishes.

Great Uncle Bill was the first to dig in, loading his plate up with heaps of chocolate pie, lemon pie, some strawberry and pretzel goop, and a slice of pecan and cherry pie.

"You're not going to eat dessert?" my mom asked me, like she didn't just watch me eat my weight in food.

"Yeah, just one small taste though. I'll take some stuff to-go."

She grabbed something off the table and joined Lara and my grandma in the kitchen. I didn't even have time to reach for the chocolate pie when Jensen, who was sitting one chair away from me with no buffer, moaned ridiculously loud. "Hmm. This is so good. So smooth and creamy. Sweet and a little salty."

"Kinda like your attitude?" I mumbled just loud enough for her to hear me.

She smiled. "It sure brings back some good memories." She closed her eyes and took another bite, then pulled the fork between her hot pink lips, like she was giving head. "It's missing something, though. Whipped cream, maybe? Yeah, that's it." She looked at me with a snobbish grin and said, "You should taste the pie. Tell me it doesn't remind you of someone."

The fact that she was eating pecan pie like it was a dick told me all I needed to know. It was David's favorite, and I was sure, if given the opportunity, Jensen wouldn't hesitate to tell me she was his favorite blow job. Everyone knew she and David had an affair our first six months together, but that shit was water under the bridge. Or so I'd thought.

I slammed my fork down on my plate a little too hard with a loud *clang*. "You know, Jensen, you aren't

the easiest person to like—never have been, actually—
and I've always, *always*, been more than nice to you."

"Really? Have you now? Because I do recall *you*
were the one who took *my* boyfriend away from *me*."

"You can't be fucking serious. Boyfriend? If you
recall, you were his side-bitch. You fucked him *after* we
got together. That hardly counts a boyfriend status."

"I saw him first."

"You mean you wanted him first and he rejected
you. Why are you bringing this shit up now? Still? Get
the fuck over it, Jensen."

"I have my reasons. You'll find out soon enough."

"Ya know, I really don't give a shit anymore. But
I guess since you're still so hung up on him, you can have
him now. He's on the mantle."

Great Uncle Bill stood up, saying something about
going to get a cup of coffee.

Jensen gently sat her fork down and dabbed her
mouth on a napkin.

"What the fuck is your problem? It doesn't usually
take you this long to move on from someone. You made
that clear by screwing Chloe's ex."

She made an exaggerated surprised look. "I did?
Who?"

"You know exactly who I'm talking about.
Derrick? Y'all work together in the same fucking office."

"Oh," she said. "Him. That was a one-time thing."

"Aren't they all?"

She stood up and leaned over the empty chair
between us. "Since you seem to know so much, then I
guess you already knew David was going to leave your

ass, you stupid bitch. We were together for the last year before he died. Where do you think he was going on all of those business trips? Atlanta?"

"You're lying. I had him last, and you can't fucking stand it. Tuck your bitchy tail, lick your wounds, and leave me the hell alone. Christ." How could I even respond to her anymore? David was dead and there was no way to prove any of it. It wasn't like I could just ask him if he was screwing my cousin…again. Getting up and walking away from her would have been the mature thing to do. I smirked instead. She was full of shit and I was calling her bluff.

Then I felt the sting of her manicured hand slap me across my face.

Someone shrieked from the kitchen.

Everything turned red and my vision blurred as my blood pressure shot through the roof.

Uncle Bill mumbled, "Holy shit," from behind me.

Instinctively, I grabbed my cheek and fought every urge I had to wrap my hands around her throat and choke the life out of her.

"Oh, for heaven's sake," Grandma Lily said, as she tried squeezing her tiny body between my mom and Aunt Lara, who both looked like deer in headlights standing in the kitchen. "You two never could just get along, could you?"

Get along? Oh, this was beyond *not* getting along. "Grandma!" I raised my voice in her direction. "Stay out of this."

My mom grabbed Grandma Lily and pulled her back. Aunt Lara shoved her way around them and came up behind Jensen.

I clenched my teeth so hard I could have cracked a tooth. I stood up and got in her face. "Fuck. You. Jensen. You are nothing but an entitled piece of Mississippi River trash whose only purpose in life is to suck any remotely lukewarm dick."

"Rowan!" my mom shouted. "You watch your mouth."

Aunt Lara grabbed Jensen's arm. "Jensen, let's go."

"I'm not finished." She smiled and licked her lips. "You know what? You and David were meant for each other. You both got what you deserve, and if you were half the nurse you pretended to be, he might still be here."

Then, just when I thought the redheaded cunt had delivered her final blow, she came out of nowhere with one more surprise. She pulled her cell phone out of her back pocket, scrolled through it, turned it around, and showed me the screen.

I almost hit the floor.

It was a picture of David...naked...in our bed.

"Wha—? Those are my sheets!" I reached for her phone, but she jerked it away.

"Trust me, you don't want to know all the dirty details. Seems like your perfect little fantasy life wasn't all rainbows and butterflies after all."

David wouldn't do this to me. No fucking way.

"Jensen Devereaux Stone. You need to be quiet."

"Did you know about this, Aunt Lara?"

"No! Of course not, Rowan." She looked at Jensen. "Really? Were you having an affair?"

"Doesn't matter anymore. *Now* I'm leaving."

"The hell you are," I said to her. As Jensen spun to leave, I wrapped my hand around her hair and yanked her back. She stumbled backward, as I reached over and scooped up a handful of gooey dessert from Uncle Bill's plate and smashed it directly into her perfectly made-up face.

"What the fuck," she squealed and spit. *Mental note, thank Uncle Bill later for his perfectly timed dessert of choice.* Her arms waved around. "Let me go you fucking whore."

Aunt Lara tried grabbing Jensen's swinging arms and got smacked in the process.

"Whore? *Me*, the whore? You fucked my fiancé! None of this would be happening if you'd just kept your legs shut!" I shoved her head forward, forcing her directly into Lara.

Jensen turned to look at me, but before she said a word, I balled up my fist and hit her square in the face. She let out a yelp and fell to her knees, clutching her face as blood, mixed with cherry pie, dripped down her shirt onto the hardwood floor.

I wiped my pie-covered hands on my pants and headed straight to the bathroom while everyone ran to rescue Jensen. I'd already decided by the time I reached the bathroom, if she called the cops on me, I was pleading temporary insanity. Surely after hearing my side of the story, the law would side with me.

Lyndsay Marie

The entire afternoon felt like a dream. It was my first family gathering since before David died. It had been hard enough doing life without him; now Jensen, my own goddamned cousin, dropped that bomb.

After washing my face and hands and cleaning myself up as best I could, I gained what was left of my dignity and made my way to the living room in search of my things. It was time for me to get the hell out of Dodge.

I pulled my purse and coat out of the pile of mixed winter accessories stacked high on Grandpa Franklin's old recliner. God rest his soul.

"I cannot believe you did that." My mother appeared out of nowhere, loaded with ammo, ready to let me have it.

"Me? My own cousin sleeps with my fiancé—twice— and you can't believe what I just did?" My mother always had a knack for somehow turning things on me.

"I certainly raised you better than this."

"Better than what, Mom? I dedicated too many years of my life to that man, and I've been carrying around this guilt for not being able to save his life, only to find out it was all bullshit anyway. And you can't believe me? Classic."

"You watch your mouth with me. And what makes you think you can just go around swinging your fists at people?"

"Oh, for fuck's sake. It's not like I'm some street fighter. Give me a br—"

"She had it coming, Anita," my grandma said behind me.

"Grandma," I said, stopping her from getting involved. "You don't have to."

"What? Take up for my favorite granddaughter? Of course I do. Don't tell me to stay out of this. You're in my house."

My mother threw her hand over her chest in an over-dramatic gesture, as if she were so shocked. *Oh, puh-lease.* "Well, I never! Rowan Vera was *not* raised that way, and I—."

"Yeah, well, I can sure as shit tell you one thing, Anita. You didn't raise me, and I've been around the block enough to know when someone has a hit like that comin' to them. You don't just go around sleepin' with other women's men and then go flash their naked pecker up in their face, rubbing it in like that." Grandma Lily looked at me. "I made you at to-go plate. Don't forget it."

SIXTEEN

Rowan

After I told everyone goodbye, I sat in my car, letting the seat heat up my butt. I couldn't believe my afternoon. Of all the shit that could have possibly gone down, learning that David had another affair with Jensen was the nail on the coffin for me.

As I sat there trying to make heads and tails of my life, a text from Wesley came through saying he hoped I was enjoying my family time and to check my email whenever I had the chance. I let out a borderline hysterical laugh. His timing couldn't have been more perfect. I told him I was having a total blast, opting to leave out the drama. I opened my email app and tapped on the first unread message from him. It was a round-trip plane ticket to Chicago flying out…in two days? *What the what*?

Me: Wesley Miller! What have you done?

I could only imagine how expensive a last-minute flight to Chicago was, assuming he booked it last minute.

Wesley: What? I told you I wanted you, so I'm getting what I want…If that's okay?

His message was followed up with a winking face and devil emoji.

Me: Of course it's okay! It's perfect. You're perfect. You are just amazing.

Okay, my response might have been a little overkill, but it was the only thing I could think to tell him at the moment because *I love you, please marry me* seemed extreme. But after the shit I'd been through, it didn't sound all *that* crazy.

Then it hit me. I was going to his home to invade *his* space. He'd already been all up in my business and seen my house a complete mess—dishes in the sink, laundry stacked on the back of the couch, bed a disheveled mess—but now I was going to *him*. I had no idea what kind of life he lived. He really could have been a serial killer living in a single-wide trailer for all I knew.

I drove the short distance from Grandma Lily's house to mine. As soon as I walked through the door, I called Katie.

She answered after a few rings. "Hello, lover. How was dinner?"

"Well, I think I broke Jensen's nose for having an affair with David! And I'm going to Chicago in two days!"

The line went silent. "Kat. Say something."

"Wait. You, did what? Why are you going to Chicago?"

"I just found out Wesley is flying me to spend the week with him."

"Okay, wow. First, take a deep breath…and a toothbrush. I can't imagine if he's flying you there at such short notice, you'll need much else. Maybe some clean underwear…or none at all." She laughed.

"I swear if I could throw something at you through the phone, I would."

"Just go and have fun and stop overthinking it."

I took a deep breath in and blew it out. "You're right. I'm sorry. How's your day going?"

"A lot better than yours apparently. I'm at my parents' right now. You want me to come by in a bit and help you pack? Plus, I'm gonna need to hear this Jensen story in person."

"I hate you in the most loving way possible, and yes, come over. The sooner the better. Drive safe, though. The roads are wet, and it's supposed to freeze later."

"'Kay. See you soon." She disconnected, and I shot Wesley a quick text asking what I needed to pack since I'd not only never been to Chicago, but I'd also never been anywhere as cold, either.

Wesley: Just bring your sexy self…and a jacket. It's cold. We'll handle the rest when you get here.

Wesley: I don't plan on us spending a whole lot of time outside of my condo…or bed.

I could only imagine what he had planned for us, but I didn't need to guess, because his next text left little room for me to wonder. *Ooh! Hello.*

Wesley: We're going to spend all of our time between the sheets, skin to skin. Me deep inside of you. You screaming my name while I bend you over the back of my couch.
Wesley: My dick is hard just thinking about you.

Judging from the picture he attached to his last text, he was not lying.

Me: Plane leaves in two days.

My body was even more thankful that he'd booked an early-morning flight. The ache I felt between my legs was too much. I replied back to him with my own picture that left no room in his imagination for just how much I'd missed him.

♡♡♡

Thank God for Katie and small favors. She left her family's farm early and came straight over to help me pack mag suitcase and split a bottle of wine.

I caught her up on my Jerry Springer-style dinner which left her just as confused as me.

"Wait, so you're telling me that David—*the* David Williams, your one and only soon-to-be-husband—

cheated on you with fucking Jensen? Jensen Stone? There's no way. No fucking way. I don't buy it."

"Believe it, Kat. She had a naked picture of him. He was in our bed!"

"I still refuse to believe it. How do you know it wasn't from when they were together the first time?"

"Because," I said, defeated. "He was laying spread-eagle on the sheets I picked out."

"Oooh, shit. I'm sorry, Rowe."

"Me too. I can't believe I didn't know. How could I have been so stupid, Kat?"

She gave me a quick hug. "You're not stupid. There's no way for you to have known."

"If you say so." I hoped she was right. I wondered if anyone else knew and had been making a mockery out of me.

"I say so," she said, trying changing the subject. "Okay. So, you're going to Chicago. When are you coming home?"

I checked my itinerary. "One week."

"Unbelievable. You are going to have so much fun. Just please, be careful. I don't like the idea of you being so far away that I can't help you if you need it."

"I'll be safe. Promise. I just can't wait for Wesley to fuck all of this drama out of my mind."

"Cheers to that."

We finished off the bottle of wine, and sometime after eleven, she passed out on my couch. I covered her with a throw blanket, then hauled myself to my own bed.

I sent Wesley a good-night message telling him we'd have to skip our nightly video chat and scrolled up the picture he sent me earlier. The image of every solid inch of him filled my screen. That was the last thing I saw before I closed my eyes and let my hands take over.

♡♡♡

I'd never been to Chicago, but apparently it was really freaking cold there…like two feet of snow on the ground, subzero temperatures cold. The last time I checked the weather forecast, it was sunny—ha! —with a high of three degrees and more snow on the way later in the afternoon. I guess if I was going to be snowed in anywhere, Wesley's place seemed like the best place to do it.

Katie dropped me off at the airport with more than enough time for me to grab a coffee and a blueberry muffin from Starbucks and flip through the latest *HGTV* magazine until it was time for takeoff.

Thankfully, the flight was uneventful without any delays. We touched down, and my insides went haywire as I waited for the plane to park. I turned off my cell phone's airplane mode, and it went out of control with new notifications. A handful of texts from Katie and Chloe came through, wishing me luck, to have fun, and not to get pregnant. One from my mom saying Jensen would be fine in a couple of days. Nothing had broken, just swollen all over, and both her eyes were black. *Fucking good.* She had it coming

I sent Kat and Chloe the same "Thanks. Just landed. Will check in again soon. Love you" text, told my mom I was sorry, again, then sent Wesley a quick

154

message letting him know the plane had landed and we were taxiing to the gate. He responded instantly that he was already waiting at the baggage claim.

When the seat belt light turned off, everyone stood to collect their bags from the overhead compartments. Wesley booked me first class, so I was in the first group of people off the plane.

I followed the signs and navigated my way through O'Hare to the baggage claim. The more I thought about it, I probably should have just packed a carry-on and dealt with the rest later…or planned to stay naked for the next six days.

As soon as I stepped off the escalator and rounded the corner, I practically slammed into Wesley. He bent down and scooped me up into a hug that lifted my feet off the ground. I wrapped my arms around him and held on as he spun me around.

He buried his face into my neck, kissing it. "God, I've missed you so much."

"Me too," I said as he squeezed me tight, "but I can't breathe."

He pressed his lips to mine as he sat me back down. Kissing him felt like the first time all over again, and I didn't care who was watching or that we were in the middle of a rush of people trying to leave the airport. Let them all watch. I was exactly where I wanted to be.

"Come on," he said. "Let's get your bag before they send it back. I need to get you home."

The drive to his downtown condo was less than a half hour, and very comfortable. With one hand on the steering wheel and his other wrapped in mine, he pulled my hand to his lips and kissed my knuckles while never taking his eyes off the road. "We're almost there."

We exited the interstate and snaked our way through the skyscrapers of downtown Chicago. "This city is insane," I said with my face pressed to the window, my breath leaving little circles of fog.

"Yeah, that's one way of putting it," he said. "I've lived here my entire life. Grew up in the burbs just outside of the city limits and moved downtown during residency. Things are pretty mellow right now because it's winter. People try to avoid going outside this time of year."

The snow continued to fall as we pulled up to a black-mirrored high-rise and turned into an underground parking garage. It was like Vegas all over again. A far cry from the single-wide I'd initially feared.

He pressed a button on his key chain and a huge metal gate slid open. We parked in a numbered spot by the elevators, and when he turned the car off, the doors automatically swung up to open.

"You ready?" He held out his hand to mine.

"Yes." *I think.*

He scanned his key card on the elevator and a few seconds later we were climbing our way to the top. He wrapped his jacket and arms around me. "You're shaking."

"Just a little cold, I guess." I'd been so lost in my own thoughts I didn't even realize I'd left my jacket in the back seat of his car.

"Let me warm you up, then." He hovered over me, backing me into the elevator wall, taking my mouth with all the force and possession I'd missed.

156

I hooked my fingers around the collar of his shirt in a death grip and pulled him into me. His hands slid around and cupped my ass as he pressed his *very* unmistakable erection into me. Just as he leaned into me, the elevator dinged as it came to a halt. He pulled back and stood up tall. "We're here."

The doors opened into a private foyer that led directly into Wesley's condo. As we stepped inside, I was taken aback by the expansive space. Everything was clean and modern but without the sterility of harsh straight lines and cold metal. It was rustic industrial and felt very warm and welcoming. "Your place is stunning!"

"Thank you," he said, as he headed towards his massive open kitchen. "You hungry? Thirsty? Would you like a glass of water or something stronger?"

"Water would be great. Please." I followed behind him and sat down on one of the bar chairs at the granite kitchen island.

He slid a glass of water across the counter in front of me. "My mom was a professional interior designer, mostly commercial. It has my mom's name all over it. She insisted on a total remodel. I haven't had the heart to change it."

"She did amazing work. I wouldn't change a thing."

"Yes, she did," Wesley said, pouring himself a glass of water. "And thank you." He walked around the kitchen island, spun my chair around, and wedged himself between my legs. He bent down and kissed my neck, his lips cool and wet from the water he'd just sipped. "Let's go get to know each other even more, but with less talking."

"You read my mind."

SEVENTEEN
Rowan

After round three or four of Wesley upholding his promise that we wouldn't spend much time out of his bed, he informed me we actually did have to get out of his bed...for an annual party one of his friends was hosting *tonight*.

"Tonight? You didn't mention anything about attending a party in any of your texts."

"Must have slipped my mind."

"Riiight. And what kind of party is this that supposedly slipped your mind?"

He massaged his hands up and down my back. "It's just a party my friend Daniel has every year after the holidays have come and gone. It's his way of getting people he knows together that wouldn't otherwise celebrate or don't have family here or don't particularly like their family and need a reason to drink after spending time with them. Overall, it's just an excuse for a bunch of people with entirely too much money to dress up in fancy shit, get together, and throw down."

"Sounds like fun but I didn't exactly bring anything to wear to a party. Much less anything fancy." Except that LBD Katie insisted I pack. I turned over to face him, his delicious naked body on full display.

"We'll figure something out. Don't worry."

"You know," I said, tracing my fingers over the ridges of his abs, "I did bring your favorite little black dress."

He grabbed my wrist and held it still. "That sounds naughty, and you're not wearing that dress tonight. Or in public, ever."

"Aw, come on. Where's the fun in that? I thought you liked it naughty?"

He pulled my hand over my head and rolled on top of me. "The naughty part comes after we get home."

♡♡♡

Out of nowhere, my life had become a whirlwind of emotion. I'd been in Chicago with Wesley for less than two full days and had more sex with Wesley than I had in the past two years. I wasn't even sure I was going to be able to walk straight after him. Now I had to go to a party and meet his best friend and God only knew who else. And what was he going to introduce me to them as? New random friend who saved his life? His girlfriend? Because I wasn't his girlfriend, but we were definitely more than friends. I'd never had a *friend* deliver as many orgasms as him. He was going to break me before the end of my trip.

160

Wesley also told me not to worry about what to wear to this party, but that didn't change the fact that the only dressy thing I'd brought with me was that stupid black dress. One that he already made clear was not going to be worn for anyone else or outside of the bedroom.

"What's on your mind, babe?" he asked as he wrapped his arms around me.

I nestled into him. "I didn't plan on going a party. You told me we were going to spend most of my time here in bed." I blew out a sigh. "Okay, so I know you didn't mean that *literally*, but still." That seemed like just as good of an excuse as any.

He kissed my neck. "Rowan, I told you not to worry, I said I'd take care of you. So here." He held out a red satin dress on a hanger in front of me.

"What? What is this?"

He let out a soft laugh. "Um, it's a dress…? You hate it, don't you?"

"Hate it? Are you kidding? Wesley, it's stunning!" It was beautiful and looked expensive.

I spun around to face him. "Thank you, Wesley. Thank you for everything."

"You're very welcome. You're worth it. Go try it on and make sure it fits." He rubbed the back of his neck. "It was a guess about what size to buy, but the sales lady suggested I go with something that had a little stretch to it, just in case."

I took the dress from him and held it up. It was long-sleeved with a deep scoop neck and slit up one side. "Okay, I'll be right back." I ran into the bathroom to try it on. Not because I was modest, but because I enjoyed making him wait to see me in it until after I was completely dressed up, with my hair and makeup done.

"You look absolutely stunning. I'm glad the dress fit you." Wesley reached across the middle console of his car and pulled my hand to his lips.

"Thank you, again." I turned to face him. "I absolutely love the dress. You have no idea how much it means to me. And you, too. You look amazing."

He didn't say a word. He just flashed one of his panty-dropping smiles.

We arrived at Daniel's place, and my stomach twisted in knots. Wesley must have sensed it because he pulled me against him as we rode the elevator up. "Relax. Everyone is going to love you. I promise." He kissed the top of my head. "They're very friendly people. Sometimes too friendly. I've already warned Daniel to be on his best behavior."

"As long as you remember who I'm here with and who's taking me home at the end of the night…and who I'm wearing this dress for." I snuggled into him under his arm, and he smiled at me in the reflection of the elevator door. I drank him in from head to toe. The man had an amazing sense of fashion. He was dressed in all black: black silk button-down, black dress pants, black shoes, and just for fun, contrasting red socks and a tie that matched my dress. "Plus," I added, "I'm not wearing a bra. So, if you need a reminder of what's yours, feel free to cop a feel anytime you want."

And that's exactly what he did…right as the bell chimed and the elevator door slid open.

Wesley wrapped his arm around me and pulled me into him as we walked down the carpeted hallway. He walked into Daniel's condo like he owned it, and the first person he introduced me to was his brother, Warren. Warren was tall and lean and just as wickedly handsome as Wesley. If I ever had to choose between the two based on looks alone, I'd be in a ton of trouble. But, based on what Wesley had told me about him being uptight, like he had a stick up his ass, I was thankful I'd met Wesley first.

As we made our way around Daniel's massive condo, Wesley introduced me to a handful of his friends whose names I'd never remember. He only ever referred to me by my first name with the added tagline, "the beautiful woman who saved my life." Never as his girlfriend.

"Did you tell anyone how we really met? Or just that I was there when you...you know?"

He kissed my temple. "No. I didn't tell a soul how you fell into my arms at a bar. I told them you saved my life." That answered my question as to where we stood.

A man's voice hollered across the room. "Wes! My man!"

"Daniel! Hey. What's up?" Wesley stepped forward to meet him and shook his hand. He wrapped his other arm around me. "I want you to finally meet Rowan. Rowan, Daniel. Daniel and I work together in the ER. He was with me in Vegas and helped me find you. He's also the douchebag I was warning you about."

Daniel smiled as he reached out to shake my hand. I took his hand in mine and shook it. "It's nice to finally meet you, Daniel. I've heard a lot about you."

"I bet you have. I'm sure whatever you've heard is probably true. Glad you two could make it."

Wesley looked around. "Seems like you had another nice turnout this year."

"Every year," he said. "I'm gonna go refill my drink. You two feel free to make yourselves at home. We'll catch up in a bit and do celebratory shots." He gave Wesley a pat on the shoulder and walked away.

"So, *Wes*? Not *Wesley*?"

He looked down at me. "Yes. That's what everyone calls me. Or Dr. Miller. Only my mother ever called me Wesley."

"Oh. Sorry. I wished I'd known. This entire time I've been calling you by a name only your mother called you? Why haven't you corrected me?"

"Don't worry, babe. I love it when you call me Wesley. As a matter of fact, I prefer it, and you'll be the only other person to get away with it."

We danced and drank the night away and mingled with some of Wesley's co-workers and former med-school classmates. For as many years as I'd worked in medicine, I'd never hung out with any doctors outside of work. Overall things seemed to go about as good as I could have expected, if not better. Except I'd become known as the woman who'd saved Wesley.

"I'm going to go get a refill," Wesley said in my ear over the music. "You want one?"

"I'll take anything you're giving me...*Wesley*."

"I can't wait to get you home and out of this dress." Then he smacked my ass and walked away.

I stood alone on the far side of the room, sipping my mix of melted ice and alcohol, and watched him from across the room as he moved with ease around Daniel's kitchen. I could have stared at him all day and night. The man was pure perfection.

Daniel said something to Wesley that caused him to look up with a hard expression on his face. I followed his gaze across the room and saw Warren deep in conversation with a petite blonde in a skintight black minidress. I could only see her from behind, but it was the first time I'd noticed her since we'd arrived at the party. I'd also been locking eyes with Wesley most of the night, so there was a decent chance she slipped in earlier and I totally missed her. I wanted to think she was with Warren, but he looked very uncomfortable talking to her.

No sooner had I glanced back in Wesley's direction than he was already gone. Good. Maybe he was finally making his way back to me with my drink, which I needed because my cup was bone dry.

My heart sank when I realized Wesley had made his way over to Warren and the mystery blonde. He had his arm around her shoulders, as he spoke into her ear.

Don't panic. They were just friends. He was going to bring her over here or come get me and introduce us. I waited for what felt like an eternity, standing awkwardly alone in a crowded room with my empty cup. Then they were gone. All three of them. They weren't in my line of sight or in the kitchen, and I was one hundred percent sure they weren't heading my direction. I tried to keep my head on straight. There was no need to jump to any conclusions. Nope. Not yet.

Finally. Someone I recognized. I stomped toward him in my heels, careful not to bust my ass on the concrete floors.

I tapped him on his shoulder. "Daniel."

He spun to face me. "Oh, hey, Rowan."

I folded my arms across my chest. "I need to find Wesley. You see him around?"

"Not for a few minutes. Last time I saw him he was with Ashley. You might want to hang back from those two."

Daniel's eyes darted around the room. "Just cause."

"Is there something I should be worried about?" It felt like the open room was closing in around me.

"No." His voice was unsure. At least that was how I heard it. "They can't be far. Feel free to explore."

My whole body relaxed with his permission to look around without having to ask. But that didn't change the fact that he warned me to steer clear of them. "Thank you."

Walking around Daniel's condo, it felt like everyone was watching me, waiting to see what the out-of-place girl was going to do about her *date* disappearing with another woman. Here I was, the plus-one at some party where everyone knew everyone, except me, and *my* date was with *Ashley*.

I casually walked around the living room, skirting around people who were dancing and drinking. The balcony was empty except for two random smokers.

When I was confident that neither Wesley nor Ashley were in the main living or kitchen area, I made my way down the hallway away from the crowd. The music faded, and everything went pitch-black except for a light blazing from the bathroom, which was empty. All of the other doors were closed, so I opened them one by one, peeking inside. Closet, laundry room, guest room—also dark, quiet, and seemingly empty—another closet, and finally the master bedroom.

The door opened with a soft *click*, and I peeked inside. Light poured across the room from what I'd assumed was the master bathroom. Soft voices carried out, except I couldn't make heads or tails of the conversation.

I tiptoed on the soft carpet and peeked around from behind the dresser. It *was* Wesley and...*her*. His back was to me, but they were standing toe to toe. I wanted so badly to yell *"what the fuck are you two doing?"* then throw something at the back of his head. Instead I backed out of the room, like a chickenshit, and quietly closed the door behind me, instead.

I'd seen enough.

I strode back down the hallway with my head held high, out into the loud music, and marched straight up to Daniel. "You ready for those shots?"

He choked back his drink, almost spitting it out. "I thought you'd never ask. Brown or clear?"

"Don't care." Far as anyone was concerned, I was still waiting on Wesley to bring me my refill from almost a half hour ago, but he was too busy holed up, doing whatever the hell he was doing, in Daniel's bathroom with fucking *Ashley*. I felt so stupid.

"Tequila it is." He set down two shot glasses and filled them up. "Did you find Wes?"

I cut my eyes to him. "Something like that. Now let's do this." I grabbed a glass and before I had time to toss it back, I felt a warm hand on my lower back.

"I see you two are getting along."

Ohmigod. That voice. That annoyingly sexy voice. I wanted to slap him and fuck his brains out at the same time.

"Hey, Wes. We were just—"

Wesley cut Daniel off midsentence. "About to get my girlfriend plastered? Yeah, I see."

I spun around to face Wesley as he pulled me into him. "Come. We're ready to go."

"First of all, I'll let you know when I'm damned well good and ready to go. And second, I am *not* your girlfriend."

He raised an eyebrow as he locked eyes with me, holding my gaze. "Stubborn woman. You want to challenge me on that second part right here and now?"

Did I? I wasn't sure. Hell, I wasn't sure of anything anymore except that being pissed off at him was damned near impossible. My mind flashed back to him and Ashley together. He even smelled faintly of her, or someone feminine.

I tried pushing him back, but he wouldn't budge. "I'm not having that conversation with you right now, *Wes*. Now I'm ready to go."

Lyndsay Marie

He told Daniel he'd be in touch, and to let Warren know we were leaving early. He tucked me under his arm and pulled me into him. "It's Wesley."

EIGHTEEN
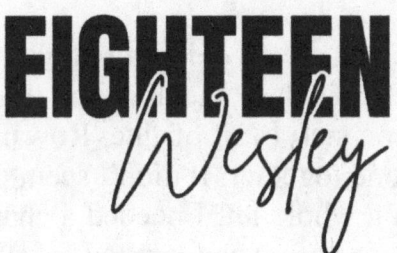
Wesley

Rowan looked like an angel in the passenger seat next to me. As mad and probably drunk as she might have been, she was still perfect. I wanted to grab her and pull her toward me, but something told me she wanted her space. I didn't know exactly what set her off at the party, but I hoped that whatever it was, one, never happened again, and two, we could work through it…when she sobered up a little. Talking to her like this would be like talking to a pissed-off brick wall.

An absolutely stunning brick wall.

I brushed her dark hair behind her ear and caught glimpses of her beautiful face in the glow of passing streetlamps. Her eyes blinked open a few times as she fought to stay awake. Her long, black lashes touched her cheeks when she closed her eyes. All I wanted to do was get her home, strip her down, and hold her in my arms for the rest of the night.

But I knew we had so much to talk about. Well, at least I did, anyway. So much bullshit, demons, things I'd kept buried. Ones that I'd hoped could stay in the dark forever. I knew, though, that if I wanted to go anywhere in life with this woman, I needed to come clean to her about all of it.

Even if that meant doing it tonight.

My gut coiled at the thought that maybe, just maybe, by some sick twist of fate, Rowan had seen me and Ashley alone together. It didn't seem possible, but it would explain a whole lot. I needed a chance to explain everything to her before she jumped to any conclusions. Something told me I was too late for that.

What the fuck was Ashley thinking just showing up at Daniel's tonight? Oh, I know. She showed up because of my ignoring of her attempts to reach me by phone, and her persistence to speak to me and not take a hint. I guess *I'm not interested—fuck off* wasn't clear enough. I should have handled her the first time she texted me that we needed to "talk in person."

She'd been drama since day one, but I chose to overlook it as a personality flaw. I didn't know I'd eventually become the epicenter of her real-life circus reality show she lived.

I made one more turn, clicked open the gate, and parked in my assigned spot. I looked over at Rowan. She'd smooth passed out. So much for awkward silence—it was sleeping silence.

I got out and made my around the car, carefully opening her door, catching her as she tipped out of the seat, all one hundred pounds of her. She mumbled something along the lines of putting her down, she could walk. That got a small laugh out of me.

I carried her in my arms as we rode the elevator to the penthouse. When we made it inside, I gently laid her down on the couch. Before I could even stand upright to sneak away and grab a blanket to cover her, she woke up.

"Who was that girl at the party?"

NINETEEN

Rowan

My head pounded as I sat up. He didn't answer my question. "The girl? The one you were all cozied up with in Daniel's bathroom? Who was she?" By God, I wanted some damn answers.

He didn't even try to cover up who she was. "That was my ex-girlfriend, Ashley Fletcher."

"Your ex, huh? You didn't feel the need to introduce us?"

"No, I didn't. I wanted to get rid of her just as fast as she showed up. If I'd known she was going to drop in unannounced, I would have had her stopped at the door. Better yet, we would have stayed home."

He walked into the kitchen as I sat on the arm of the couch and kicked off my shoes.

Wait. Ashley *Fletcher*? Suddenly, I felt like I'd been hit by lightning as recognition of her name sank in, remembering the text he got when he was at my house. Things started clicking together. Then I wondered if he'd been seeing her since he'd been home. "Wait, what?"

173

How could he just talk so casually about her showing up like it was nothing? And he wanted to hide her from me? "I know what I saw in that room."

"What?" he asked from behind the kitchen counter where he filled up a glass with water.

Even in my current state of anger and inebriation, he still looked like a fuckable work of living art. "Just exactly how do you expect me to react to the fact that you wanted to hide your ex-girlfriend from me, and then I walk in on her pawing all over you?"

"Rowan, it's not what you think."

"It's not? Enlighten me then. And was that the first time you've seen her since you were in Memphis with me?" Because the last thing I wanted to deal with was trying to start some new, long-distance relationship, only to turn around and find out I already had to worry about his ex-girlfriend making unwelcomed and random guest appearances whenever I wasn't around.

He rubbed his hands down his face.

All I wanted was to be pissed off at him, but he made it so damned hard.

"Look, Rowan. There's a lot of history there that you and I haven't even scratched the surface of, yet. You want a glass of water?"

"Please," I said as I flopped down on the oversized sectional and curled up under a flannel throw blanket. "Looks like I'm gonna need it."

This didn't strike me as the kind of conversation we should be having under the influence, except Wesley acted like he was stone-cold sober. Though it was a little too late now. He'd just opened Pandora's box.

174

He handed me a glass full of water and an aspirin. I downed half of it and took the little white pill.

He sat down beside me. "So," he started. "That was Ashley, as you already know, my ex-girlfriend." He stretched his legs out in front of him, laid his head back against the back of the couch and closed his eyes. "We were together for a lot of years. Three months after my transplant, she surprised me with her pregnancy. I was fucking thrilled. We were going to have a baby; I was going to be a dad." He softly laughed.

He had a kid? With *her*? Shit just kept getting better and better.

"Then—" He took a sip of water and continued. "—we went to her first ultrasound appointment. There are no words to describe that feeling of seeing your first kid for the first time and hearing that little heartbeat. But something wasn't adding up when the technician did the baby's measurements and I saw the profile of the baby's face on the screen. Then she gave us an estimated due date, confirming what I already knew. Ash was around the sixteen-week mark, which meant she got pregnant sometime in late October. I was sicker than shit, in the hospital waiting to have a heart transplant. The only other time I slept with her after that was the end of January. She wanted me to believe she got pregnant in January and was only a few weeks along when we went to her doctor's appointment."

I swallowed hard and fought back tears. I placed my hand on his cheek against his soft stubble. He kissed my palm. "Wesley, I'm so sorry." I didn't know what else to say. My heart broke for him. And God only knew what I'd have done if David had knocked up Jensen.

"Oh, just wait," he said. "It gets better…or worse. The entire ride home from that appointment, she couldn't for the life of her understand why I was so quiet, how my mood had all of the sudden done a one-eighty. I thought, there's no way she's that stupid or thinks I am. But she did. She thought she was going to get away with it. I mean, hiding her pregnancy was the easy part. I was in the hospital, and we'd spent most of our time apart. Of course, I confronted her as soon as we walked through the door. She just stood there with nothing to say because she knew I was right, and she had no logical explanation or argument. That was the end of us. I packed her shit and sent her on her way right then and there. I didn't even ask who the father was, and she didn't offer. It didn't matter and I didn't care. It was already too late. But when she left, she didn't go to her mom's like I expected her to. Oh no. She ran straight to Van Buren." He leaned forward and rested his head in his hands.

I couldn't see his face, but I could only imagine the pain he felt having to relive this nightmare. I wanted to kill her myself.

I rubbed my hand over the tense muscles across his back. "Why would she run to your dad? Did she think she could win you back through him?"

Wesley sat back and looked me dead in the eye. "No, Rowan. She went to him because he's the father of her baby."

All the wind was knocked out of me. "What the fuck? Are you serious? Your girlfriend slept with your dad and got pregnant by him? While you were in the hospital?" Suddenly everything Wesley told me about his family and broken relationship with his father made sense. But this was not what I expected at all.

"Yeah, it's a whole tangled web of drama and not something I talk about to just anyone. Actually, I haven't told anyone. I prefer to block it out. But considering us"—he gestured between me and him— "I thought it needed to be out in the open, so you'd better understand me and why things are the way they are. Van Buren did me a favor because I would have married her if she hadn't gotten pregnant. Who knows what would have happened if I hadn't learned who she really was or was dumb enough to believe that baby was mine?"

"Seriously, what is wrong with people? I'm sorry, Wesley. That's really shitty."

"I've all but written both of them off. He finally gave up trying to contact me a couple of months ago, which is fine by me. I don't want to see him, her, or their baby." He laughed and shook his head. "I can't fucking believe at thirty-six, I have a baby brother."

None of this explained why she'd just showed up unannounced tonight or what her intentions were when they'd disappeared together, alone into a bedroom. "What did she want tonight? Wesley, I walked in on you and her practically doing God knows what in that bathroom. That hurt like you wouldn't believe."

"Rowan, I have nothing to hide from you. Trust me. You have no idea the feelings I have for you already."

I was relieved to hear him say that. And the truth was, he had no idea how I felt about him already.

"I don't know what exactly you saw back there, but I assure you, it's not what you're thinking." He brushed a lock of loose hair from my face and tucked it behind my ear. "I haven't seen or heard from her since the day she left. Until Vegas. That was the first time she tried reconnecting with me. I avoided her like a plague, so showing up at a party she knew I'd be at was her only way to talk to me in person. She knew better than to show up here or my work."

"What was so important that she needed to see you?"

"She came there to tell me my dad recently found out he has cancer. Best I can figure is he gave up trying to make contact me once he found out. That's when she started trying. Then she proceeded to tell me she still loved me, and she'd made a mistake. She wanted another chance. Then she tried to kiss me. What you didn't see was me pushing her away and telling her to fuck off."

Holy. Shit.

If I wasn't sure before, I was one hundred percent convinced that I loved him already or, at the very least, was well on my way.

"Look, Rowan, I'm sorry she showed up tonight. I had no idea she'd do that. It never crossed my mind. But please, don't let that ruin our entire night, or any of our time together." He held out his hand, waiting for me to take it. "She means nothing to me anymore. Nothing. Not now, not ever again. When I put her out that door, it was with every intention of never seeing or talking to her,

178

ever. Hell, you're the first woman I've even remotely talked to or slept with since her."

I put my hand in his, and he pulled me deeper into his chest, wrapping me in his embrace. "You're forgiven, Wesley. And I'm sorry too. This is all new to me, and I'm just not sure how to navigate yet. I don't know what I'm doing."

He leaned down and softly pressed his lips to mine. It was gentle but filled with need and desire. His warm hand slid across my leg and under the thigh-high slit in my dress.

"Just keep doing what you're doing, babe. We'll figure it out together. You know," he said, "I believe I have it in writing somewhere that I was going to bend you over the back of my couch."

I swallowed hard. "I believe you did say that."

He reached behind my back and unzipped my dress. We kissed as his hands slid across my bare skin peeling the dress down. My dress dropped to the floor when he stood and lifted me off the couch with him. I wrapped my legs around his waist and fumbled with the buttons on his shirt, trying to get him at least half as naked as he had me. He walked us around and carefully sat me on the back of his couch. "I got it. You just sit and hold on."

As he stood in front of me, he proceeded to undress himself. His fingers moving slow and methodically. First, he loosened his tie, laying it across the back of the couch. Then he unbuttoned his shirt and dropped it to the floor, exposing his naked, chiseled upper body. He kicked off his shoes and socks and finally his pants and stood there in front of me like some kind of delicious, forbidden treat, his erection pressing hard against the silky material of his boxers.

I wanted to reach out and touch him, taste him from head to toe. Instead, I gripped the back of the couch with one hand to balance myself and spread my legs open. I pulled the lace material between my legs to the side and touched the wetness with my free hand. He licked his lips and dropped his boxers to the floor. I panted, out of breath as I rubbed harder, knowing he was watching me. That was when my feet slipped on the wood floor and I'd lost my balance, flipping feet and ass in the air, up and over the back of his couch, landing upside down between on the area rug the couch and coffee table.

He ran around the couch and stood over me, gloriously naked. "Rowan. My God, are you okay?"

"I'm fine. Probably should have just stuck to bending me over."

TWENTY

Rowan

"Ms. Honeycutt, I'm terribly sorry for your loss. I'll be just outside your room. If you need anything, please call."

My loss. My loss? *She had no idea about loss. Two hours ago, I had someone talking to me about donating David's organs. He'd managed to make it to the hospital, but in the end, death won. Now he was somewhere in the same building as me, laid up in a hospital bed, waiting for me to give the word to pull the plug. Then an hour later, another doctor was elbows-deep in my vagina, examining me for a* lost *pregnancy. A baby and a fiancé were not things you just* lose. *Those are not things to be misplaced and found at another time.*

I sat in the hospital bed for days in a catatonic state staring down at my stomach, pissed off at the world. Pregnant? *Who the fuck knew? I sure as hell didn't.*

"Rowan." A soft, distant voice called my name. "Rowan, baby. Wake up. Please." A hand shook me gently. "Rowan, please, baby, wake up."

I was startled at the sight of Wesley lying on his side propped up next to me. "What the hell?" I was drenched head to toe in sweat. At least that's what I'd hoped it was. "What's going on? What time is it?"

"You were having a nightmare." Wesley's voice was soft and sad. "It's two thirty, babe."

"I'm sorry. I...the dreams haven't been coming back near as often as they used to. I was hoping I'd get through this trip without having one. Did I say anything?"

His eyes searched mine. "A little."

I bit my lip. "How much did you hear?"

"That depends. How much are you willing to share with me?"

I was never really ready to talk about my life with David. I turned to face him, our naked bodies touching. Since Wesley had opened up to me about his past, I broke down and told him all the painful details about mine. We'd talked a about some of it before, but not like this. I opened up about my dad's suicide, which I hadn't talked to anyone about in years. My broken relationship with my mom. I told him everything about the first affair my cousin Jensen had with David and then told him what I knew about their most recent affair and how I'd lost my shit and attacked her at our family gathering.

He laid next to me, silently listening as I told him about David's and my wreck, my miscarriage that night because of said wreck, and finally about him being an organ donor, and my therapists' idea to reach out to the society that coordinated his case so I could finally seal this vault forever and move on.

Wesley still hadn't said a word. I must have sounded like a total whack job, but he needed to know what he was getting into before thinking about committing to me in any way, shape, or form.

"Wow," he finally said.

Wow about summed it up. All my demons laid out before him. If he didn't run before, he would now.

"Jesus, Rowan. I didn't know you were a street-fighter."

I smacked him on the arm. "Oh, you just wait and see then. You're in for a real treat."

He smirked. "I highly doubt that. But I am so sorry for everything that's happened to you. But I'll start by saying one thing…"

"What's that?"

"I think you know, more than anyone, that I know exactly what it feels like to hold yourself responsible for someone's death. But you also know more than anyone that you cannot carry that weight with you forever. Even if it was your fiancé." He kissed my forehead. "There's a lot of emotion to sort through in that scenario, but I will say this and give you one less thing to worry about."

I sighed into his chest. "What's that?"

"You said David was an organ donor."

Every muscle in my body tensed at his words. I told him that as more of a side note than a topic of interest I wanted to keep discussing. "Yes. He was."

He ran his fingers through my hair. "Well, just based on everything you've told me, I'm willing to bet, deep down, you are terrified that by some impossible chance, because I had a heart transplant the same month he died, you're worried that he and I are somehow connected? Am I right?"

Yup. He was. And it really was an impossible chance, but still a chance. I mean, look how Wesley and I had found each other. "Yes. It scares the shit out of me, as unlikely as it is."

"Well, I can assure you, Rowan, we are not connected via heart transplant, only by you. I told you Vegas was a pit stop between Hawaii and home. I was actually in Hawaii meeting the family of my organ donor. The unlucky guy was stateside on a business trip, fell asleep at the wheel. He was actually driving to the airport to head back home. I was already in the hospital when they got the call. Now, here we are."

I blew out a sigh of relief. Knowing that gave me a whole lot of closure I didn't realize I was needing.

"Thank you, Wesley, for everything, and telling me your story too. I really needed to hear it."

"Anytime, babe. I'll always be here for you."

Then, for seemingly no reason at all, the waterworks busted wide open.

Wesley pulled me as I ugly cried into his chest. "Everything is going to be okay. If there's one thing I can promise you, you'll never have to worry about me sleeping with your cousin."

The last thing I remembered before dozing off was being tangled up from head to toe with Wesley.

I woke up with a jolt in a pitch-black room to the smell of freshly brewed coffee. Since there was zero light in the bedroom, I hadn't the slightest clue what time it was. As I stretched out., I rolled over, then snuggled into the soft, satin sheets. It was a nice change from having to peel myself out of the comfort of my warm bed and make coffee myself. Too bad I only had a few days left of Wesley's personal room service.

Male voices carried into Wesley's bedroom from outside the door. The only one I recognized was Wesley's. I threw on one of Wesley's T-shirts and a pair of my pajama shorts and slipped out into the living room. Wesley was standing behind the island in the kitchen barefoot and shirtless, wearing only a pair of jeans, while his brother, Warren, sat at the bar across from him.

Warren pointed and Wesley turned to face me. "Good morn—well, afternoon, sleeping beauty. Coffee's fresh."

I snuggled into Wesley's half-naked body and looked up at him. "Good afternoon? What time is it?"

Warren laughed. "One thirty. Asshole here only woke up because I showed up when he didn't respond to any of my phone calls or text messages."

It was nice to know they had each other's backs, but damn, one thirty? Wesley and I had finally fallen asleep sometime after eight this morning, so it made sense we slept half the day away.

"I was just catching him up on everything that went down last night. Nothing we need to talk about, again. I feel like you and I said enough last night and this morning."

I pressed up on my tippy toes and kissed his soft, full lips. "I agree. I'm going to get some coffee. Thank you for making it."

He smacked my ass as I walked away. "You're welcome. Help yourself to some breakfast too, or call it lunch if that sounds more appealing."

"All right," Warren said as he stood up. "I'm going to leave you two lovebirds alone. I just wanted to make sure you were okay."

"We're great. Thanks for checking in. I'll walk you out."

"Nice meeting you, again, Rowan. We'll all have to have dinner before you leave. Something a little quieter with less drama."

I smiled at him. "I agree. It was nice meeting you."

"Come on, let's go," Wesley said as he guided his brother toward the door. I watched him like a hawk as he stalked out of view. I wanted to bite his ass through his jeans. I didn't know how two people had managed to create brothers who were damned near perfect, but the Miller boys were it.

A ceramic tray of fresh cut fruit, bagels, and cream cheese sat on the counter about two feet from my face, teasing me. My stomach let out a long, rolling growl as I eyed the food. As much as I still felt like a stranger in Wesley's house, hunger won. I grabbed a bagel, spread some cream cheese on it, and bit into it.

Wesley walked up behind me and wrapped his arms around my waist, pulling me into him. He was rock hard. *Hello, Houston. We no longer have a problem.* "Eat up, babe. I need you to restore your energy."

I dropped my bagel. No point in trying to eat with him pressed against me. "Yeah. Sorry about drinking so much last night."

He trailed kisses from behind my ear down my neck to my shoulder. "No need to apologize. You were having fun."

"Hmm. I did." Until looney chick showed up. "Speaking of alcohol, how is it you recovered so fast? You don't even seem fazed by any of it."

He pulled his T-shirt I was wearing up and over my head and threw it somewhere behind him. His warm hands caressed my skin, across my back, then down my hips, where he pushed the waistband of my shorts down until they fell to the floor around my ankles. He slid his hand around front and rubbed the wetness between my legs, teasing me, slipping his fingers agonizingly slowly inside, then pulling back out.

I bent forward, gripping the black-and-white marbled countertop.

"I recovered," he whispered in my ear, "because I don't drink alcohol, Rowan." I rocked against his hand.

That was news to me. Someone who didn't drink? Didn't matter. I had his hand between my legs and was going out of my mind.

He stopped moving, and I let out something that sounded like a cross between a moan and a whine. "Can I help you with something, babe?"

Oh, there was. "Wesley. I want you inside of me." He had me completely naked, bent over the cold kitchen counter, as he stood behind me, teasing me. "I want you to fuck me. Now, please."

I heard the unmistakable sound of his zipper as he stripped out of his jeans, and then the firmness of his

warm cock replaced his hand, barely breaching my
entrance. I was dying to get him inside me.

He grabbed my wrists and spread my arms out
until my chest was pressed flat against the cold
countertop. "Don't worry, I'm not going to let you fall,
again. But whatever you do, do not let go. If you do, I
will spank you."

Warm liquid trickled down the inside of my
thighs. *Holy hell*. The thought of him spanking me did
not sound like a punishment at all. In fact, I wanted to test
him and let go. Just to see what he'd do.

He gripped my hips as I clung tight to the edge of
the counter. Then slowly he pushed inside of me.
"Remember. Don't. Let. Go."

"Okay," I whispered. I wanted to turn around and
see him, to look into his dark and daring eyes. But he
wasn't having it. I was at his mercy.

He pulled out and right when I was about to lose
my mind at his absence, he thrust forward and slammed
into me as hard as he could. My feet left the floor, and I
struggled to keep my grip. *Shit*. Now I knew why he'd
warned me.

He repeated his moves, over and over—pull out,
then *slam*—as my feet rose off the floor. My hand, slick
with sweat, came up as I lost my grip trying to keep
myself from sliding forward. I thought he hadn't noticed
until his own hand came down on my bare ass with a
punishing *smack* at the same moment he slammed deep
inside me. "Holy shit, Wesley. I'm so close." Then, out
of nowhere, he stopped. "Goddamnit, Wesley. You're
killing me here," I said, just as he spun me around.

He bent down and gave me a soft, gentle kiss on my lips. "You are so beautiful, Rowan. I mean it."

I closed my eyes and savored the delicate way his lips touched mine.

"Stay right here and keep your eyes closed," he ordered with a firm, easy tone.

Obeying his command, I stood with my back against the kitchen counter, bracing myself for God only knew what. It didn't take long for me to feel his touch again. This time, he traced a finger gently over my mouth. My tongue darted out to try to catch his finger, but it was already gone and moving down my neck.

"Hmm, chocolate?" I asked as his finger traced along the edge of my breast and down my stomach, causing me to flinch.

"Frosting." His finger circled underneath my belly button before reaching its final destination between my legs.

I rocked forward into his hand but was instantly greeted by his tongue, which he used to retrace the path of his finger in reverse.

Fuck. My. Life.

Everything he did was mind-numbing torture and seduction at the same time.

He faintly kissed my lips. "Come."

My eyes fluttered open. "What do you think I've been trying to do?" I said with a smirk.

He smiled back and took my hand. "I meant with me. Climb on up." He hopped up on the island and carefully pulled me up with him. He was still hard as a rock. I could have sat there and spent all day just drinking him in like ice water on a hot summer day. Instead of wasting any more time dreaming about what I could do to him, I straddled him. I rocked my hips, sliding back and forth along his firm length, until he finally found his way inside of me.

"I want *you* to fuck *me* now, Rowan."

That's exactly what I did. When I was sure he'd come, and he knew I had too, I collapsed on top of him. "Nice touch with the chocolate frosting." I planted a kiss in the middle of his chest. "It might just be my new favorite."

♡♡♡

"Ugh." I huffed facedown into the pillow. It was my last day with Wesley before catching my flight to Memphis sometime tomorrow. We'd spent most of the rest of our time together naked in his penthouse, with the exception of dinner last night with Warren and Daniel. No one brought up any of the party mishap.

"What's the matter, babe?" Wesley asked, rubbing his hand up and down my back.

"I'm not ready to go home."

He rolled over and stared up at the ceiling. "Me either. This has been one hell of a week with you."

That was an understatement.

I propped up on my elbow and faced him. "I'm sure we'll see each other again soon. It's not like I'm so busy I have to schedule you in."

He wrapped his arms around me, pulled me down, and kissed me. Soft and slow, then hard with a lot of tongue.

God I was going to miss this. I was going to miss him. I wanted him and what we had, every single day.

"Then don't leave."

I laughed. "Right. I wish, but it's not that easy."

"Why not?"

"Because...I have a life in Memphis." It hadn't always been the best, but it's where I was born and raised. I'd never considered leaving it forever. Except that one time when I threatened to run away when I was fifteen.

He looked me dead in the eye. "I'm serious, Rowan. At least, if you have to, then come back...and stay."

What? Did he just...? "Wait. Wesley. What are you asking me?"

"I want you to move in with me."

"What?" I almost yelled. "Are you serious?" I looked around the room for cameras. This had to be one of those *caught on camera* shows. Someone was going to jump out of the closet and yell "gotcha".

He shot up and pinned me down to the bed, holding my arms over my head. His mouth crushed to mine. There was no doubt, I loved kissing Wesley. He kissed me unlike anyone I'd ever kissed before. He also fucked like no one else and was about to prove it.

So, he was serious. Holy fuck. We barely knew each other, yet I actually considered his offer. "You really want me to move in with you? Like, live here every day?"

His hard dick lay heavy between my legs. He pressed forward, nudging me open. I gladly obliged, and he slid inside of me.

"Yes," he whispered in my ear. "I'm serious." Slowly he slid out and paused, then thrust forward hard and deep. "I." *Slam.* "Want." *Slam.* "You." *Slam.*

"I want you too," I choked out as my body jerked underneath him. He pulsated inside me as his own orgasm took over.

TWENTY-ONE
Wesley

I was so totally fucked over Rowan. She consumed every corner of my mind from the time I woke up until the time I closed my eyes at night, and every moment in between. There had never been anyone in my life who I'd booked a last-minute flight for just to spend one or two nights with, only to come home, work a few shifts and repeat.

Hard to believe an entire week with her had come and gone. *Poof. Up in smoke.*

"What's on your agenda after I leave?" she asked, pouring herself another cup of coffee. Who knew the act of someone refilling a ceramic mug could be such a fucking turn-on? Because I sure as hell never got that memo. But it was and I had the proof.

I took a sip from my own cup. "Well, a lot less sex, for starters."

She grinned. "Self-love still counts as something."

"Not the same." I'd done enough self-love ever since I first laid eyes on her. Surprisingly, I had a dick that still worked after the use I'd gotten out of it. "Come here while I still have you." She rounded the kitchen island and wedged herself between my thighs. I took her cup from her hands, set it down, and pulled her into me. Then I kissed her like my life depended on it. Because in that moment, it felt like it did.

She broke our kiss, wrapping her arms around me while running her tongue across my neck. "When did you say my flight left?"

A low growl escaped me. "Too soon. I need to have you at the airport by four."

"Hmm. Sounds like we have plenty of time for at least two more rounds."

"Indeed, we do." It took every ounce of self-control I had in me not to yank that shirt over her head and bend her over the kitchen island right then and there.

"Three if we push our luck. But I need to run downstairs to Warrens for a few minutes, first. I shouldn't be gone long. You're welcome to go."

"As much fun as that sounds, I need to eat and take a shower. I'll be ready for whenever you get back."

Maybe I didn't need to go see my brother as much as I thought. No. I did. I'd make it a quick trip. I stood and pulled her in for one more kiss that left both of us breathless. "I'll be right back."

"Aren't you just going down a few floors?"

"And?"

She pushed my shoulder playfully and strutted into the kitchen. I caught myself trying to sneak a peek under the back of my shirt that hung just below her ass. "And? You act like you're leaving me forever. I'll be waiting right here. I'm going to make an omelet. You want one?"

"That sounds amazing. Wait until I get back to make mine. I don't eat cold eggs."

She flicked her hands, shooing me toward the door and told me to go. I was being kicked out of my own house. I liked it.

♡♡♡

The elevator descended the two floors down to Warrens floor. He probably thought I'd lost my mind texting him at six this morning that I was coming down in a bit and to be decent in case Rowan came with me.

After a few minutes of friendly conversation, he turned all *stick in the ass* brother. "So what exactly, are you going to do about this girl?" Warren's hand waved upward as if to gesture toward my condo, while giving me a "don't say anything stupid" look, because he knew I was about to give him what he'd consider a stupid response. The pretentious bastard.

"Rowan, you mean? Jackass." *Refer to her as this girl again and I'll knock your ass out* was what I wanted to say, but I had enough respect for my little brother not to actually hit him. "She and I still have a lot to work out." Like getting her to Chicago—permanently—because I needed her here with me. Not because I couldn't afford to fly back and forth on a whim...every day if I wanted to. What I didn't need was her meeting someone else by some unnatural coincidence the way she'd met me and then dropping me like a bad habit. Chances were slim, but I couldn't risk it.

"Well, I hope you know what you're doing. You've only known Rowan, what, a few months?"

I gave him a stare that challenged him to come up with something else. Our parents knew each other for thirty days before getting married. "Your point?"

This coming from the man who hadn't had a steady woman in at least five years. Not that I'd kept tabs on his love life, but he was no fucking professional when it came to relationships.

"My point, asshole, is you don't know jack-shit about her and you're already in way over your head. Rowan seems like a very sweet girl, but did you already forget about what Ashley did to you? Or do I need to remind you?"

"Fuck off, dude. First of all, Rowan isn't a girl. I assure you; she is all woman. Second, she isn't Ashley and don't ever compare the two. You've been around them both. Clearly, you see the difference between the two. What I have with Rowan is contrasting on every level, so no, you don't need to remind me of anything. If *you* recall, Ashley was, or is, a cheating whore, and the fact that I can literally hop on a plane at any given time, show up at Rowan's front door without warning and know I won't walk in on her riding some other dude's cock, speaks volumes about her. Don't you think?"

He stared at me, not responding. It wasn't my fault he couldn't find a decent woman out of the millions who were out there. I'd even tried to set him up a few times, but he refused.

"I'm sorry," he said. "I crossed a line. I shouldn't meddle. And you're right. It's not fair to compare her to

Lyndsay Marie

Ashley. I'm sure Ashley has been a shining beacon of a faithful housewife to Dad."

"Yeah, I'm sure she is. And thanks, I appreciate your support."

"I wouldn't call it support, but you're a grown-ass man. I can't tell you what to do."

"Good," I said. "Because I asked her to move in with me."

He just shook his head. "Is that why you came here to ask for the key to mom's old storage unit?"

I knew Rowan *liked* me, and if I was lucky? She'd love me sooner rather than later, if not already. I knew how I felt about her, even if it was too soon. Way too damned soon. And that key went to a lock that held the contents I needed to prove it. "It is."

His expression was impassive, but the wheels were turning. If he thought about it any harder, smoke would have shot out of his ears. "Fine. On one condition."

"What?"

"You know what the hell you're doing."

That was debatable. "Always."

TWENTY-TWO

Lyndsay Marie

TWENTY-TWO
Rowan

I couldn't believe my time with Wesley was about to be up. Seven days disappeared in the blink of an eye. Despite the one dramatic hiccup at Daniel's party, the trip was not a bust.

I glanced at the microwave clock above the stove and sighed. He would be taking me to the airport in a few short hours. I could have just as easily said 'yes' and taken him up on his offer to leave my life behind and start fresh with him, but it didn't feel that easy to do. Could it be? Just pack up life as I knew it and kiss it all goodbye?

I put a pan on the stove, sprayed it with oil, and fired up the gas burner. I milled around Wesley's kitchen while the pan warmed up, gathering ingredients to make an omelet. The burglar alarm panel by the door beeped, alerting me the front door had opened. "That was fast," I said with my back to the door, while I mixed up a couple of eggs and chopped veggies. I spun around and almost dropped the glass bowl and egg mixture. "Who the hell are you?"

199

Standing less than twenty feet front of me was *her*...holding a baby. She smiled brightly, effortlessly. Like she was supposed to be here. The morning sun beamed behind her, creating this white aura around her. The baby cooed and she readjusted him on her hip. "Ashley! I tried calling Wes, but he didn't answer." Uh, ya think? He's been avoiding you for how long now?

"We've been...busy. H-how did you get in?" My stomach turned and I felt like something was going to projectile out of my body one way or the other and would probably resemble the beat-up eggs I was holding.

"Oh, I still have the code and a key." Her words were nonchalant, like, *it's no big deal. I do this all the time.* She looked around. "Wes isn't here, is he? I really need to talk to him."

"No. He isn't." Okay, floor, you may open up and take me at any minute now. Ha. Ha. Universe. Joke's over. "Didn't y'all talk enough at the party?"

She rolled her eyes. "I tried. He didn't want to hear anything I had to say. Too many people around. Wes is very private. He hates having personal conversations in public areas."

I'd say so. So private it seemed like he'd failed to mention a few things. Like, why in the hell his ex-girlfriend still had access to his home.

Her baby made some loud squealing noise that got her attention. She said something to him about being quiet and his daddy would be home soon. "Silly me. I didn't introduce you to little guy here. What did you say your name was?"

Lyndsay Marie

I didn't. "Rowan." I didn't tell you my name, or to get the fuck out, which was also on the tip of my tongue. The urge was strong with the latter.

"Rowan," she repeated to herself quietly. "Well, Rowan, this is Weston Asher." When she switched Weston to her other hip, his face came into full view. I've watched a lot of Maury Povich in my days, but it would take a hella ton of DNA testing to convince me of the words "you are *not* the father". Even though the Miller boys' genes ran strong, Wesley had some major splainin' to do.

Christ on a cracker. I was ninety percent naked, fighting off the urge to tackle this bitch to the ground, as this cute, dark-haired, dark-eyed baby, who looked just like Wesley, as he wiggled in his mom's arms.

"Ashley." I forced her name out of my mouth. "I don't really think there is anything I can do for you. Like I said, Wesley isn't here." And fuck? How long had he been gone? Ten minutes at least. He had to be on his way back up.

Ashley cut her eyes to the door and back at me. "Actually, there is something you can do for me. Tell Wesley he's behind on his child support. I need some money. Taking care of his son isn't cheap."

Son? So he *did* lie to me? No way in hell I wanted to believe her, but she gave me the answer to my question before I had a chance to ask it. Why, though? Why not just tell me on the front end he had a kid instead of making up some elaborate story about his dad and her? What else had he lied about? Did he really have his transplant when he said he did? Because if not, then that kid most definitely could be his. I know men lied about having kids all of the time, so it wasn't out of the realm of possibilities.

"All I wanted was a little of his help. That's all. I gave up asking for him to be in our lives a long time ago."

I huffed and slammed the bowl of eggs on the counter with a little too much force. *Get it together. She is full of shit. Don't let her under your skin.* I folded my arms over my chest, careful not to let my shirt ride up in the front—or she'd get a peek at what Wesley had been looking at all week—and shifted to face her.

"He clearly didn't tell you anything about me. Hell, I'm not even sure what he tells anyone, but it seems like it might be a little far from the truth." She wiped baby drool off Weston's chin. "You didn't know about Weston, did you?"

Bingo! You're a real Captain Cbvious, aren't you? I couldn't wait for Wesley to get home to clear this shit up, because the longer I stood in her presence, the harder it got for me to keep from flying across the room and tackling her to the ground. Just add that to my record. *Rowan: two-times champion of living room brawls.* 'Cause I'd definitely win against her. But she had a kid in her arms, so that made things a little tricky.

"When did he stop?"

"What?"

"Paying you? When did he stop paying you your child support?"

She closed her eyes for a minute. Ashley was definitely pretty. She had the whole down-to-earth, take home to your mama, homecoming queen, probably

202

attends church every Sunday and volunteers at the homeless shelter, doesn't even need to wear makeup, look about her.

She finally spoke. "He hasn't made a payment since last November."

November? But that's when we—ohmigod! Did he stop paying her because he met me?

"Rowan, he abandoned us. Threw me out the door while I was pregnant with *his* baby." She looked at the front door as if she were remembering the day it happened. "All I ever wanted was to know why? And why did he stop helping me out and if he will again?"

My empathy meter kicked up a few notches. Maybe it was the tears in her eyes or that sweet little baby she held that supposedly belonged to my lover. I swallowed hard. "I'm sorry." What else could I say? I didn't want to help her. I couldn't help her. This was beyond anything I could control.

She looked at me, and the expression on her face changed from disappointment to almost crazy. Like she had some kind of revelation and a switch flipped. "Was it because of you? Did you do this?" She stormed towards me and stopped just a few feet away. "Did you tell him to stop paying me?"

I backed into the counter as far as I could. "Me? Wha—no! Why would I have anything to do with that?" Hell, up until this point I thought Wesley's father was her baby daddy. No need in telling her that, though. She'd probably drop the kid and come after me.

She backed off. "I'm sorry. It's been hard enough without him in our lives."

I blew out a sigh of relief. That was a close one. "I think you need to go now." Tears blurred my vision, but I refused to let them fall. She was not about to storm her ass up in here and ruin what'd been the best week of my life by throwing around accusations.

"Yeah, you're right. Sorry for barging in on you. Wes doesn't usually have company. I'll try again later."

I'd lost all hope in, well, everything, as she left, and the front door closed. It was impossible to feel any ounce of confidence while standing in the middle of a kitchen in a home that wasn't my own, wearing only a T-shirt—also, not mine—all while learning that what I thought was a fresh start at life was turning out to be another big fucking lie.

A hint of smoke hit my senses. *Shit.* I'd forgotten about the pan that was heating up! I shut off the burner and set the blackened frying pan in the sink, rinsing it off with cold water. The condo reeked of a burning smell.

Rather than stand around trying to figure out how to cover up the putrid scent and wait for Wesley to get back from Warren's, I decided then it was time to go. I got dressed and packed up the rest of my things in record time. Once I'd convinced myself I was making the right decision by leaving early, I scribbled a note to Wesley on a napkin apologizing for the smell and left.

...

My phone blew up with calls and text messages from Wesley less than two minutes after I buckled myself into the backseat of an Uber heading towards the airport. My timing for leaving couldn't have been better because if weren't for me having already had most of my shit packed, Wesley would have walked in on me, and I know for a fact I'd be naked underneath him by now.

I didn't respond to him or answer his calls. Instead, I called my mom. Of course, she didn't answer. So I left her a voice message. This was one of those times a girl just needed her mom, even if we weren't close.

At the airport, I made it through security and to my gate with more than ample time to kill. I sat in what would eventually become the terminal I would vacate from on a one-way flight home. The airport was bustling with travelers—families, businesspeople, the lone traveler—flocking in waves, rushing to their next destination. It was easy to tell when the captain of a plane gave the *all clear* to exit. As the people around me boarded their plane, I was, once again, left sitting in an empty terminal. Staff probably thought I'd missed my flight. Nope. Just sitting here waiting. Forty minutes down, four and a half hours to go.

As I stood up, contemplating which retail space or restaurant I wanted to invade first, someone called my name from close behind.

"Rowan. Wait."

I sucked in a deep breath and spun on my heels, facing the man I wanted to escape. "What in the hell are you doing here?" He went to reach for me, and I shoved his hand away. "Don't touch me."

He had a pained look on his face, like I was the one who'd hurt him. *Sucks, doesn't it?* "Rowan, please. Can we just talk?"

I examined his eyes for the truth. Something. Anything that would reassure me that *talking* was going to do either of us any good at this point. "Talk? You want to talk? I think I've heard enough talking for a lifetime."

"Then can we at least sit down? People are starting to stare."

"Good. Let them. You probably want a witness." Maybe that was a little harsh. I wasn't actually going to inflict harm on him, and hopefully, he knew that. But I was beyond pissed off, even though he smelled and looked delicious. Damn it, brain, focus. Anger—engage!

He tried grabbing my hand, but I pulled it away. He retreated, walked to the far side of the gate, and sat down in a chair in an empty row against the wall. It'd become a stare-off between us—me standing in the middle of the room, his back to the wall, neither of us saying a word—and he won.

I walked over to where he was and sat down one chair away. Space was exactly what I needed. Not him trying to hold my hand or lean in for a kiss. Not that he had tried to kiss me, but I wouldn't allow him to distract me with his sexual powers.

Then, he assumed the same position he did the night he told me all about Ashley—leaned back, legs crossed and stretched out in front of him, arms folded over his chest. So, if there was one thing I'd learned about him was he had a stance when he had something important to say. I just didn't know if what he was about to tell me was the truth or a lie.

"I saw Ashley."

I rolled my eyes. "Huh. Yeah, me too. She seems sweet." Or really fucking crazy. I'd yet to finalize that opinion.

"You don't understand, Rowan."

I leaned across the middle seat toward him. "Then fucking enlighten me, Wesley!" I accidentally yelled. I cleared my throat, and before I spoke another word, I took a deep breath and lowered my voice to a pissed-off whisper. "She was there. In your condo. Barged in on me half-naked while I was making *our* breakfast."

He scrubbed his hands down his face. Then he sat up and took my hand. I tried pulling it back, but his grip held strong. "I am so, so fucking sorry she did that. Will you please give me sixty seconds? Just listen?"

My foot tapped against the leg of the chair at a rapid pace. "Fine. One minute."

"Thank you," he said, relieved. "I don't know what she told you, but I'd venture to guess that none of it was true. What *I* told you about our past is truth. You can take that to your grave. I went to Warren's to get something from him and when he went to get it for me, he saw her crossing the street, leaving our building. I blew out of there so fast; I couldn't get to you quick enough. By the time I made it home, it was too late—you were already gone."

What the hell was I supposed to say? Okay, you're forgiven? Let's move on like nothing happened? None of what he'd said explained anything. "So at what point during your sixty seconds are you going to tell me that Weston is yours?"

He drew back with a confused and disgusted look on his face. "Weston? Who the hell is Weston?"

I threw my hands in the air and stood up. "Oh, come on. You shitting me right now? Weston Asher? Your son?"

Wesley stood up, grabbed my shoulders and spun me to face him. He had fire in his eyes. An emotion I'd never seen with him. "Rowan, that is not my kid. I didn't even know his name until you said it just now."

I wanted to believe him. So much. Unable to hold eye contact with him, I looked to the ground between us. "Wesley. I-I can't do this with you." As much as I wanted to be with him, it would never work unless I took that leap and actually moved in with him. It'd be the only way he could prove to me any of what he said was true.

"Does this cut into my minute? Because I think my time is up."

I nodded. "Time's up."

He dropped his arms from his hold on me, backed off, and walked away.

TWENTY-THREE
Rowan

My phone rang as soon as I walked through the door. Damn. I could not catch a break. After the shit I'd been through with Wesley at the airport, I was done for the day. Maybe even the rest of the year.

An old familiar name popped up on the screen. My heart sank.

John Williams. It was David's dad.

We hadn't spoken in months, and that was mostly because his wife, Tess, hated me. Hated with a capital *H*. John had always sided with me, but it was hard for him to keep in touch with his wife, Tess, always up his ass. I debated letting it go to voicemail since we hadn't spoken in so long because I couldn't even begin to imagine what he wanted from me now, and I didn't have the emotional capacity to talk to him at the moment.

Screw it. Let's just sprinkle some salt on the wound.

"Hey, John," I said as I answered his call.

"Rowan. It's Tess. I knew if I called you from John's phone, you'd answer."

What the? Tess? "Hi, Tess. What can I—."

"Cut the nice shit, Rowan. We need to talk."

I took a deep breath and thought better of responding to her. After several tortured minutes of listening to her shrill voice, I disconnected our call.

"Motherfucker!" I screamed as I pitched my phone across the room. I knew I never should have answered.

♡♡♡

"Look at you, glowing and shit!" Chloe said, giving my arm a shove. "You are totally falling in love!" Funny. 'Cause falling in love was the last emotion I was feeling. It felt more like I'd fallen on my face a few times today. Probably looked it too.

After my—mostly—one-sided phone call with Tess, I sent out a 9-1-1 text to Kat and Chloe for an emergency girls' night. They were happy to oblige, seeing as they'd yet to hear much about my trip to Chicago.

"I am not," I said, trying to convince myself more than anything. It was hard *not* to fall for someone who, in just a few short months, proved he was willing to do anything for me.

"Oh, you definitely are. You're totally in love with Wesley," Katie said, teasingly. "And that's okay. You deserve it, Rowe. We're happy for you. I can't wait to actually meet him."

"Not gonna happen, y'all. So stop. Just give it a rest." My voice was loud and clipped. They both looked at me like I'd grown a second head. I threw myself back on the bed with a huff and pulled my hair.

Kat crawled up and straddled my lap. "What do you mean it's 'not gonna happen'?"

"He asked me to move in with him."

Katie didn't hold back. "Holy shit, Rowan!" she shrieked as she hopped down and stood in front of me. "You're joking? Is that why you called this emergency meeting?"

"Ha. I wish. We sort of aren't seeing each other anymore." Acknowledging the cold hard truth out loud gave me a chest pain. If I didn't know how to properly assess it, I would have thought I was having some sort of coronary event. I could think a whole lot straighter when Wesley wasn't screwing me into oblivion.

Her excitement came to a screeching halt. "Wait, did you just say y'all *aren't* seeing each other anymore?" She turned to Chloe. "Are you hearing this shit?"

All I heard was an "Um-hmm."

She rolled her eyes. "Spill it, Rowan."

I sat up and crossed my arms. "We just… we need some space. Things were moving way too fast." I gave them the very censored and condensed version of my week, including the drama with his ex—both times—and him leaving me standing alone at the airport with more questions than answers as I watched him walk away. I wiped a rogue tear that fell from my eye.

"I'm so sorry, Rowe." Kat pulled me into a hug. "I can't believe he just left you. And you haven't heard from him?"

"Nope. Not a word. He went from blowing my phone up this morning to complete silence tonight after walking away."

"Well...have you reached out to him?" Chloe asked.

"No. What's the point? Him walking away told me everything I needed to know."

Chloe played with my hair and gave it a tug. "The point is you love him. I think you should at least call him."

"I'm not calling him. Period."

"Fine. You do you, then."

I already had. I'd done me, literally, and Wesley, a hell of a lot more. *Doing me* was what got me into this mess. I bit my lip. "So, there might be one more thing."

"You're pregnant, aren't you? I told you, Kat! I knew it!"

"Seriously? What? No, Chloe, I am not pregnant." Though it wouldn't surprise me one bit at the rate Wesley and I went at it when we were together.

"Then what?" Kat asked. "Because you're just full of all kinds of exciting news."

I huffed. "Tess called me this afternoon."

"Tess?" They both looked at me in disgust. Hell, my mouth felt dirty saying her name.

I recapped our one-sided conversation because Tess had done most of the talking and wouldn't let me get a single word in edgewise, not that it would have made a difference. But in that brief time we were on the phone, I'd learned that not only was the house I'd been living in not mine, it also hadn't been paid off like I thought.

"Wait, what? So, John's owned this house the entire time?"

"Yup. Seems that way. It was left to him, and he was the executor of David's estate. David had a life insurance policy that was supposed to pay off the mortgage. Except the policy lapsed for non-payment. When David died, John reassured me he'd taken care of everything. What he was doing was paying the house note so I wouldn't know that the house wasn't actually paid off. He was just going to foot the note for as long as he could."

"I still don't get why John kept this from you, or why Tess waited so long to tell you. I mean, they've known this whole fucking time?" Chloe asked.

That revelation that John had known about it from the start broke my heart. Once Tess discovered her husband was still paying for the mortgage on a house that was technically hers, too, she couldn't resist telling me to get the fuck out of *her* house. "John was trying to protect me, I guess," I said. "The statements quit coming here because he apparently was having them sent to his work. I never thought to check on the actual deed. I had no reason to. Not until if and when I decided to sell. He hid it from Tess for as long as he could."

"So, how'd Tess find out, then?" Katie asked. "I mean, that's a pretty big secret to keep from someone for that long. And what's she gonna do with this house? She sure as hell doesn't need it."

I laughed. Not because it was funny, but because this shit was my life. It was one thing to learn that everything as I knew it had been flipped and shaken, again, but now I had to say the words out loud to my best friends, which made it real. "Tess's accountant was getting paperwork together for one of her business adventures and found the house payments on their bank statements. Of course Tess confronted John. He couldn't deny it. She had a paper trail showing where he was making my house payments. Now I have fourteen days to move. She said she already has a buyer."

Katie looked at me in shock. "Who?"

"Who else?" My tone was sarcastic. Tess's buyer should have been way too predictable. "Jensen."

"No shit?" Chloe asked.

"Yup. No shit." Tess Williams always wanted her precious baby boy to buckle down and settle with Jensen Stone. She'd made that clear. So much so that she always made sure to mention Jensen's name whenever David and I were within a hundred yards of earshot of her. David blew her remarks off like she was crazy. Little did I know, Jensen was blowing him off.

"What a clusterfuck," Chloe said. "And how shitty of Tess. All of them. I need a drink after that." She got up and went toward the kitchen.

"So, what happens now?" Kat asked, pushing a piece of hair out of my face.

That was the million-dollar question. One that didn't actually win me a million bucks. It just made my head hurt. "I move."

"Where, though? You just said you and Wesley broke things off."

I sucked in a deep breath and blew it out in defeat. "To my mom's"

"Woah. Did not see that coming" Kat checked my forehead with the back of her hand. "You feeling okay?"

"Yes!" I laughed and swatted her hand away. "She's never home. I doubt she'll notice I'm there. And it won't be for long. Just until I can get back on my feet."

"Does she even know you're coming?"

"She will when she gets back from vacation or checks her voicemail."

♡♡♡

Chloe left sometime after midnight. Once Kat woke from the dead the next day, we sat around my dining room table eating breakfast, talking about life, and basically mapping out my near future plans. Before I could even think about moving, I had to figure out what to do with twenty-five hundred square feet of house packed with four years' worth of memories. A part of me wanted to burn this big bitch down with everything inside, but it was too nice of a house, and orange wasn't my color. Instead, Katie and I drove to the nearest grocery store after breakfast and loaded up on as many empty boxes I could fit in my car. No time like the present to start sorting and packing up my stuff.

"Where do you want this?" Katie asked, holding a box in her arms.

Tess had given me whopping two weeks to vacate the premises. Why waste any more time? "Just set it in the living room by the fireplace. I already started a pile." I turned off the light and closed the door on the spare room for the last time.

"Okay, done. Where to next?" Kat met me in the hall and handed me a glass of wine.

I sighed and took a sip. "I guess my room? It's the only one left." It was the one room I dreaded cleaning out the most. David's personal belongings, and anything that remotely reminded me of him, had long been boxed up and inconspicuously tucked away in the back of my walk-in closet behind a shoe shelf. It was easy to ignore it on a day-to-day basis.

"It's now or never. Right?" *Right?* I mean, it would be like unsealing an ancient Egyptian vault, only it didn't contain priceless treasures. No, this was what was left of my life with David. Every personal belonging of his: clothes, shoes, framed pictures of us, right down to his toothbrush, toothpaste, and cologne. I had zero intentions of going through any of it. It was just the fact that I had to see his shit one more time.

Katie stood beside me and grabbed my hand. "Remember, he cheated on you. What's in those boxes is one big fucking lie."

I took a deep breath in and blew it out. She was right. I shoved the shoe shelf out of the way, and without skipping another beat, I yanked the top box down from the stack, letting it drop to the floor, and ripped open the cardboard flaps. I only needed to grab one thing and knew exactly where to find it.

♡♡♡

"Thanks for all your help." I leaned into Katie's driver's-side window on my tippy toes and gave her a hug. "You're an expert packer." We'd managed to collect, pack, and stack what few things I was taking with me to my mom's by the front door, all by late-afternoon.

"You're welcome, Rowe. Seriously, though, anytime you need me, I'm there."

"I know." I sighed. "Thank you. Love you big-time."

"Love you too."

I headed inside as she drove off to order take-out. Suddenly, while standing alone in this massive empty house, I found myself completely overwhelmed and full of doubt about my entire life, questioning what the hell I was doing with it. I thought about Wesley and about us, wondering if I should have given him the benefit of the doubt. I'd made him out to be the enemy. Yet, he still hadn't so much as breathed a word in my direction since yesterday.

While waiting for my food to arrive, I dug through my purse and pulled out the black velvet box I'd tucked away earlier and flipped the lid open. It was exactly how I remembered it, and it still fit. It took a few therapy sessions, a lot of screaming and crying, chucking random pieces of home decor across the house, a bottle of wine or two, and self-indulgence of two pints of Ben and Jerry's. But after six months, I'd finally taken it off and put it away.

217

I looked down at the light reflecting on the stone, making tiny sparkles. Then I checked my phone again for some sign of life. Blank. Nothing. Not from Wesley nor my mother, which wasn't surprising for her. Just as I was about to plop down on my couch, the doorbell rang.

I jumped up, slipped the ring off and shoved it in the front pocket of my jeans. I ran to the front door and swung it open. My phone slipped from my hand and hit the tiled entryway with a *crack*.

Lyndsay Marie

TWENTY-FOUR
Wesley

I stepped under the threshold into Rowan's house without her invitation and shut the door behind me. Ballsy move on my part considering, well, everything. I half expected her to slam the door in my face, and to be honest, I probably deserved it.

But, here we stood, just like before. I waited, hoping she'd launch herself into my arms like the last time I showed up and beg me to take her to her bedroom. Instead, she stood there in front of me, mouth wide open. Despite her temporary hatred toward me, I still wanted to feel that pretty little mouth of hers wrapped around my— *wait, no.* I wanted her. Just her. That was why I was here.

I kneeled down, never taking my eyes off hers, as I picked up her now shattered phone. "I'll be sure and get you a new one." I stood and set it down on the side table.

"Wha—? Wesley? What are you doing here?"

The conversation I'd rehearsed all night and the entire way here played over and over in my mind a thousand times. But once I laid my eyes on her, I couldn't even remember where to start. "I'm here for…you." She still hadn't moved an inch, but she didn't look mad that I'd shown up out of the blue, and she didn't try to run away. So I closed the space between us, standing toe to toe, her body almost touching mine. "Give me one chance to explain everything. Please."

She looked up at me with her teary green eyes. They flicked back and forth, searching my face. I wiped a tear off her cheek with my thumb as she exhaled, her breath hot on the palm of my hand. "Okay," she finally said softly. "Let's talk."

We walked to her couch and sat down on opposite ends. I looked around the room at the stacked moving boxes, and the slightest hint of hope passed through me, even though I knew better than to think she was waiting for me to come to her rescue. "Moving somewhere?"

She stared at her bare feet propped up on the coffee table and picked at a string on her jeans. "Something like that."

Okay, Miller. Time to nut up or shut up. Or this conversation would go nowhere fast. So, I poured my heart out to her without thinking about it anymore. "Rowan," I said, turning to face her. I grabbed her hand, and she gave me major side-eye. But she didn't pull away this time, so I took that as a small victory. "I have never in all my life felt the way about someone as I do about you. It was not some bullshit coincidence based on our horoscopes that we met. We didn't bump carts at the grocery store or meet on a blind date through a mutual friend. This is some serious shit happening between us. I know you feel it too." I squeezed her hand. "Babe, I saw you before I *saw* you. That night at karaoke I watched you laugh and dance with Katie and Chloe from the time I arrived up until the second you walked off that stage for the last time. I listened to you guys sing quite possibly the worst rendition of any karaoke song I've ever heard." She smiled a little, remembering that night just as well as I did. I continued because I didn't want to lose her. "And that little...black...dress..." I said, emphasizing every word, "left me absolutely speechless. I knew by not making a move on you, I risked losing you forever. But, by some unknown force of nature, I found you, again, at the race. Surrounded by tens of thousands of people, you were inches from me. My plan was to follow behind you to the finish line and then ask you out...but that didn't exactly go according to plan. Instead, though, Rowan, you literally saved my life. And in more ways than one." My eyes focused on hers. She let her tears fall. I did not want to see her to cry, but she needed to know how I felt about her. "And this heart," I said, pulling her hand to my chest. "Rowan, it still beats because of you, and for you. Why would fate let us meet if we can't be together? Please...I'm begging you, give us a chance."

I saw all the hurt and pain, the struggle she was facing, the suffering and the internal battle to stay and fight or let go and move on. It was the same war I'd fought with myself for a long time. But from the moment I'd met her, I knew right then it was time to knock that wall down and move on...with her. "Please don't cry. I didn't mean to..." The pain and uncertainty and fear she felt killed me on the inside, but there was so much more than that. There was love for me, and a lot of it. I could see it. I knew this would be hard for her. Fuck, it was just as much for me, but I was more than willing to open myself up and give all of me to her, regardless of the risk. She was worth it, and life without her was not. She was the reason I was still here and the reason my heart still had a beat.

"Why did you leave me? How did you just turn and walk away from me without looking back so easily. I honestly didn't think I'd ever see you again."

"Rowan." I squeezed her hand which was still intertwined with mine. "That was the most difficult decision I have ever had to make. All I wanted to do was wrap you in my arms and carry you home with me. But you—we—weren't in a place to work through things. At that point I still didn't know what the fuck was going on, and you needed your own space. I didn't want to interfere with that because I needed you to know exactly what you wanted. I just hoped like hell in the end it was me."

She sniffled. "Then where did you go?"

"Well." I lifted her hand to my lips and kissed it. "As soon as I left you, I went back to the ticket counter and bought another plane ticket. This time one with the first empty seat on the next flight to Memphis, which happened to be three hours ago, otherwise I would have been here sooner…like last night."

"Another ticket? What do you mean *another* ticket? Where else are you planning on going?"

I laughed. "Apparently Bora Bora." Her confused look made me smile. "How do you think I was able to get to you in the first place? Security wouldn't let me through to the gate without a damned ticket. So I bought one on any flight out of there."

"Ohmigod! You didn't?"

She laughed for the first time and I relaxed a little. I brushed a few strands of loose hair away from her face and tucked them behind her ear. "I know you have a lot of questions for me but before you ask, please let me explain. I promise you, you can ask me anything else when I'm done, and I will give you the absolute truth."

She sucked in a deep breath and slowly let it out. "Okay."

Thank fuck she didn't tell me I only had sixty seconds this time. Talk about pressure. "I called Ashley as soon as I left the airport. I would have called her on the way there, but I wanted to get to you first. Quite frankly, I had nothing to say to her, but she almost cost me you. I had to stoop to her level to find out what the fuck was going on." I stood up, then knelt down on one knee in front of Rowan without ever letting go of her hand. If things had been different between us in that moment, I might have popped the question to her right then and there.

Rowan seemed completely unfazed by the irony of the very uncomfortable position I was in due to the lack of space between me and the coffee table digging in my back. "I'm sure whatever she had to say was…interesting. Maybe even compared to what she had to tell me."

"I'm getting there. I promise." God only knew what in the hell that crazy bitch told Rowan.

"How did she get in like that? And to me? You can't tell me that was the first time she just showed up out of the blue because she had a key, and she seemed pretty damned comfortable in your place."

Reluctantly, I let go of her hand and rubbed my face. Then I adjusted positions but stayed on my knees in front of her. At least I knew this way she couldn't stand up and bolt. Not without kicking me in the face in the process. Though I wouldn't have put it past her. "She did not have a key. She had the elevator code. It was my fault for not ever changing it. After what we'd been through, I honestly didn't think she'd come back. But once she found out about you the night at the party, you became her new target. I left the door unlocked when I went down to Warren's. She was already there in the hallway waiting for an opportunity to catch you alone. I don't know how long she'd been there or how many other times she'd done it. That's for the police to sort out."

Rowan sat straight up. "The police? Why are the police involved?"

"Because I filed a restraining order on her. I told you she was fucking nuts. She spewed quite the array of expletive words at me when I talked to her on the phone, none of which mentioned me having a kid with her. When I hung up on her I drove straight to the police with our recorded conversation and filed a report."

She looked like she was holding back a smile. If I didn't know any better, I'd have sworn I was winning her back. "Rowan, I told you, I have nothing to hide from you. Not now, not ever."

"So that really isn't your baby? None of what she told me was true?"

I grabbed both of her hands. This time she laced her fingers in mine. "No. None if it is true. Not unless she told you she had an affair with Van Buren and came out of it with his love child, then no, babe. That is not my kid. That's my little brother."

She looked to the ceiling then back down at me with tears in her eyes. "Fuck. That's a relief. But why did you completely stop trying to get a hold of me? You went from blowing up my phone when I left to absolutely nothing."

"Because I spent the rest of my day and into the night between talking to the police, changing all of my passwords and locks, getting security to pull video for the police. It's a big fucking mess. But I'm having it taken care of. And I did text you. I just never sent them. I told you, I wanted you to have your space. If you don't believe me, you should see my draft messages."

My feet were numb and tingly. So I stood up and pulled her up with me. I let go of her hands and wrapped my arms around her. I moved just ever so slightly to keep from losing contact and planted a soft kiss on her salty cheek. "I will never, ever hurt you, ever. Not on purpose. Please know and understand that. I will do anything and everything I can, every day of my life, to prove it to you."

She looked up at me with conviction as tears streamed down her cheeks. "I know you aren't going to try to hurt me. I just can't go through that pain again. Wesley, do you understand that?"

There was nothing left for me to defend. Instead, I pulled her mouth to mine with such force I was worried I'd hurt her. She relaxed, opening up and letting me in. I kissed her with all of the passion and desperation I had left in me. She moaned when I broke our kiss. I looked her dead in the eyes. "Rowan Vera Honeycutt, I love you."

TWENTY-FIVE
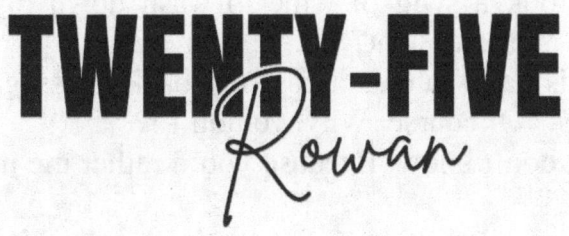
Rowan

In life, there are no guarantees, only promises we make and do our best to keep. Wesley had no idea just how much I believed he wouldn't hurt me. He had already proven that beyond a shadow of a doubt and given me no reason to question him otherwise. I wasn't even sure what I was afraid of anymore. I felt like I'd already been through the worst of it.

"So," Wesley said, with a mouthful of Chinese food. "Your mom's, huh? Are you sure that's a good idea?"

I shrugged. "Define good."

We spent the night hanging out on my couch, splitting the take-out I'd ordered because it was enough for four people, and clearing up everything that had transpired over the past few days. It was a doozy. We never did figure out his ex's motive for coming after us other than she was bat shit crazy.

He pushed his empty plate aside, kicked his feet up and put his arm around me while I kept eating. "Well, you know you better than anyone. If moving there is what you need, you have my support. I'll help you move your stuff over there tomorrow."

I took a swig of wine to wash down my food. "Really? You'd do that?"

His hand rubbed across my back, massaging my shoulders. "Of course. Why wouldn't I?"

"I don't know. Because you'd rather me move in with you?"

He smiled. "Yeah, but that's a really big move. There's no pressure on you from me. Besides—" he leaned up and kissed my neck, then my jaw, around to the corner of my mouth. "—what kind of man would I be if I forced you into doing something you didn't want?"

I pushed him back, climbed up on his lap, and straddled him. "You know what I *do* want that you don't have to force me to do?"

He gripped my ass, pulling me down into him. "Oh," he whispered in my ear, "I know exactly what you want. But it's not going to happen tonight."

♡♡♡

After Wesley's frustrating tease and iron-clad restraint against me, I decided he could still stay the night. Okay, so I wouldn't have actually kicked him out. But the thought had crossed my mind a few times. We slept on the couch in our clothes, and he was a perfect gentleman. No matter how hard I tried to convince him not to be one.

"Do you need to take a shower or do anything here before I take you to your mom's?"

Wesley helped me pack up my car with the boxes that contained what few personal things I wanted to keep, and my shoes and clothes, which, thankfully, wasn't a whole lot either. The only two things we weren't able to grab due to lack of space and manpower were my bed and my dad's desk. After checking in with Katie, she said not to worry, she'd get someone from her parents farm to come get it and store it until I had a place for them. Just to let her know when.

"No. Not unless you're going to join me…"

He smirked, causing a dimple to appear, and kissed my forehead. "As much as we both would enjoy that, I am not."

"Well, I guess I'm done, then. I think everything I'll need is already packed up. If not, I'll just buy more. I'm ready to get the hell out of this house."

"This it then?" he asked, picking up my suitcase by the door.

I looked around. "I guess so. Can you give me just a minute? I want to do one final run-through, just to make sure I have the essentials." Because my plan was to never set another foot inside this house once I locked the door.

"Of course, babe. Take your time. I'll be outside."

I'd already gotten everything I wanted to keep. When the door shut behind Wesley, I walked across the room and stood in front of the fireplace. David's ashes sat in a silver urn in the center of the mantle. It's funny, as many times as I was sure Wesley had seen the urn, he'd never once said a word or asked about it. He never asked me if I was going to take it with me or what I was going to do with it. At one point, I wanted to dump the contents in the toilet and flush it.

"You're a selfish prick, David. You really are. Jensen? Of all people. Could you imagine the family gatherings?" I scoffed. "You probably never thought that far ahead. You only thought about yourself. Well, ya know what? Fuck you. I get to have the last laugh. You and Jensen get what you wanted—to be together in your house. Have a nice life, asshole."

As I turned to leave, I pulled up the draft message I'd created for the organ donation society and hit Discard. Then, I closed and locked the front door for the final time and dropped the keys in the flowerbed beside the porch.

Wesley shoved the last of my stuff that would fit in the trunk of my car and slammed it shut as I approached. "There. All set. You ready?"

"As I'll ever be." I climbed in the passenger seat and buckled my seat belt.

He stuffed himself behind the wheel, leaned across the console, pulled me into him, and kissed me. He handed me his phone. "Punch in your mom's address into the GPS."

I took his phone and pulled up the GPS app as we backed out of the driveway and headed north without saying another word.

I watched out the window as the houses, streets, and stores I'd known for my entire life passed by. A small laugh escaped me as I thought about what Tess and Jensen's reaction would be when they walked through the house. Probably one of horror at the amount of shit I'd left for them to sort through.

We stopped at a red light just before the exit to the interstate. "Where's your mom live? Seems like were getting further out of town. I thought you said she lived close to you."

"She does." It was hard to contain the shit-eating grin on my face. "There's been a slight change of plans."

I looked over at him and he raised an eyebrow. "There has? You want to stop and grab lunch first?"

I smacked him on the arm. "Just follow your GPS."

He picked up his phone and looked at it. Then me, back at his phone, then back at me. "Rowan. This says our end destination is Chicago."

"Yup." I leaned my seat back and put my feet on the dash. "And it's a long drive."

The light turned green, and we merged onto the interstate. Wesley grabbed my hand and held it tight. "I know this isn't easy for you, babe, so anything you need, anytime you need it, please let me know. Okay?"

He was perfect with his at least three-day-old stubble. I knew he meant every word, even with his eyes hidden behind sunglasses. "Wesley, I really, really love you."

We drove in silence for a while, and as we took the last exit before leaving Memphis, I shifted in my seat to face him. "Actually, there is one thing I need you to do for me, please?"

"Anything. What is it?"

"When we get to the Memphis-Arkansas Bridge, I need you to pull over before we cross over. Just stop somewhere in the middle. Please."

Lyndsay Marie

"Are you sure that's safe?"

I laughed. He probably thought I was nuts. Hopefully, he didn't think I was going to run away or jump off. "Yes, it's safe—probably. There shouldn't be too much traffic going that way this time of day. I'll be quick. Promise."

He pulled my hand to his lips and kissed it. "If you say so."

Just as we crossed under the "Welcome to Arkansas" sign, he eased over onto the emergency shoulder and put the car in park. I waited as a truck passed by, then hopped out and walked to the guardrail overlooking the Mississippi River. I reached into my pocket and flung the last of David's memories in the form of a platinum band, into the muddy water and didn't even wait to watch it land.

The entire stop took all of six seconds.

"Everything good?" he asked when I got back in the car and clicked my seat belt on.

"Everything is perfect."

EPILOGUE

Rowan

Most nights my goal was to fall asleep before I fell apart. It wasn't even a concern of mine anymore because I got to go to bed and wake up next to the most amazing human being I'd ever known.

Except for when he woke me up to go running.

"Oh, come on, babe. It's just a little fun run. A 5K never hurt anyone," Wesley said, smacking me on the ass.

"Oh, come on babe, wah, wah, wah," I mocked him. "First of all, the words fun and run do not belong in the same sentence. Ever. Two, I told you I gave up running after Vegas. That was temporary insanity agreeing to that. And three, if you recall, that race didn't end so great for either of us," I reminded him.

We hadn't even been living together a solid three months, and I was beginning to question my decision.

"Okay, you need to move on from Vegas. That was eons ago and a fluke. It hasn't stopped me from running," Wesley said. "Besides, that race is what brought us together. So, I'd say something good *did* come out of it."

He got me there. But Wesley ran at least five miles a day at the park when the weather was decent, and when it wasn't, he was at the gym in the basement pounding away on the treadmill. I hadn't even run as far as the bathroom. Except for this morning, no thanks to the bottomless margaritas we drank last night with Warren and Daniel.

"Wesley. I haven't even speed-walked to the mailbox since we were in Vegas. If I even want to consider this, I need time to condition myself to keep up with you." The most working out I'd even remotely participated in was in our bedroom…and bathroom and kitchen and balcony.

He bent down and kissed me. "No worries. I'll go slow so you can keep up. The race is in two weeks. You have plenty of time."

Two weeks? I was screwed.

I rolled over in bed, wrapping myself in the sheets, and admired Wesley's tall, muscular, completely naked frame as he stood in front of the bathroom mirror getting ready for the day. It was in that moment I realized I'd do anything for him…even run a 5K.

♡Two Weeks Later♡

"I cannot believe I let you talk me into this shit, Wesley Miller." I looked over at him. He was standing tall, grinning from ear to ear. Why? I had no idea. Surely it wasn't for the opportunity to run a 5K with me and his brother. I knew this race was important to him for one very good reason: it raised money for cancer research, and he did it in his mom's memory. So maybe that was it.

Regardless of my preparedness, he looked incredibly edible and ready to run in his tight-fitting tank top, gym shorts, and running shoes.

He wrapped his arm around me and pulled me into his side. "Thank you for coming." Then he kissed the top of my head.

I leaned into his body and inhaled his strong, masculine scent. "You're welcome, and lucky I like you. I wouldn't do this again for just anybody."

He planted a kiss on my temple. "Don't lie. You love me."

There was no denying that. I loved him.

"Okay, you two lovebirds. Get a room." Warren's comment interrupted our moment.

Wesley raised his arm to the sky in a dramatic way. "The world is my room. Don't like it, don't watch."

Funny thing is he wasn't lying. He did not hold back in public. If he wanted to grab or smack my ass, he would. Or if he wanted to stick his tongue in my mouth and make out in the middle of the grocery store, done. He'd even pinned me against a random wall on a crowded street just so I could feel how hard I'd made him for no good reason.

"I can't believe Warren agreed to this nonsense either," I said to Wesley, more as a reminder that he talked not one but two people into running with him.

Wesley winked. "He loves me too."

The race finally started, and I, surprisingly, kept a pretty good pace. Wesley and Warren held steady beside me, occasionally falling a little behind as they talked to each other. We were only about halfway in, and I could feel myself slowing. Body parts were starting to hurt, and I had killer indigestion, but I pushed forward. I'd spent the past two weeks doing practice runs on the treadmill. So far, so good*ish*.

I found my groove and wished I had headphones with some music. I'd been wearing them while conditioning for this little race, and it was a nice change being able to run to music. But Wesley was adamantly against them in case he wanted to "talk to me" during the race. *Yeah, okay.* He hadn't said two words since we'd started running.

I hummed a little tune in my head instead and counted my steps.

One, two. One, two.

"Rowan." I heard my name being called in the distance behind me. It wasn't the volume that got my attention, it was the tone in the voice.

I slowed down and realized from the corner of my eye I'd lost sight of Wesley and Warren. They'd fallen way behind at some point.

"Rowan. Stop," I heard again. "I need your help. It's Wesley."

Everything around felt like it was suddenly caving in on me. A million memories flashed through my mind in a split second as I started to recall everything from the night of my wreck to Vegas and seeing Wesley lying on the ground and in the hospital bed, and every day and night we'd shared since then.

My body came to a sharp halt.

Life moved in slow motion as I turned around toward Warren's voice calling my name for help.

♡♡♡

"Ohmigod! Ohmigod! Ohmigod!" Chloe squealed as she practically jumped into my arms, damned near knocking us both to the ground. "I can't believe you're a married old hag now! I'm so happy for you!"

We jumped up and down with our arms wrapped around each other in the middle of the dance floor. "I know! Crazy, right? It doesn't even seem real." She let go and danced away.

I couldn't believe it either. Taking such a big leap wasn't easy, but I needed to try, to give Wesley and love a chance. It wasn't any easier walking down the aisle alone, but that's just the way it was. Warren had offered, and it was a sweet gesture, but I'd declined. I still wanted to kill him for agreeing to participate in Wesley's ploy to propose. If they'd asked me first, I would have told them that surprising me during a 5K race by telling me Wesley needed my help was *not* a good idea. But I would forever remember the sight of Wesley down on one knee holding out the biggest diamond ring I'd ever seen in my life. And what made it even more special was it once belonged to his mom. He admitted this ring was the reason he went to Warren's that day I was leaving Chicago. He knew then he wanted to marry me and had been keeping it in his pocket ever since.

Wesley was adamant about not waiting to get married. And I agreed. People have done crazier things—like wake up hungover and married in Vegas.

We flew Kat and Chloe in soon after his proposal to help me pull off the wedding of my dreams…including a dress, which was no easy feat for a lot of reasons. Between them two and the strings Wesley had pulled with some of his connections, everything went off as planned. We had a romantic wedding on the rooftop terrace at his condo, surrounded by the few people who mattered the most to us. He'd even gone as far as to invite his dad, Van Buren, who'd declined due to not feeling well because of his chemo treatments. Then Wesley had somehow pulled off another big surprise by flying my mom up with Grandma Lily in tow, after Mom had already told me she was going to be out of town the week of our wedding.

Kat stumbled over to us and leaned on my shoulder for support. "Rowan, I love you, but I should kill you for not ever telling me how sexy Wesley's brother is. That man is a God." I smiled thinking back on her reaction when they met for the first time. She said she almost pissed herself when she saw him.

Chloe didn't seem all too disappointed having to walk with Daniel, either.

"Minor details," I said, doing my best to hold Katie up. I released myself out of her death grip and held her steady. I knew the open bar was a bad idea, but Wesley insisted it was necessary. "Thanks, for being a good sport about it, but we need to get you home and to bed."

She swayed back and forth. "Nah, I'm good. I'll just Uber to our hotel."

"No way in hell you're taking an Uber alone in Chicago."

I spotted Warren across the room over Kat's shoulder, leaning against a wood column, looking just as dapper as his brother—*my husband*—watching us as he sipped his drink. Hell, he'd been watching her all night.

I waved him over to us.

"If you're gonna watch, you're gonna participate," I called out to him. "Take her home, make sure she's safe. Please."

"Sure thing, *sis*." He smiled, scooped up Katie effortlessly in his arms, as she squealed and giggled at his gesture, and carried her away.

I hiked up some of the hundred pounds of wedding dress and made my way over to the minibar.

Wesley's smooth, warm voice came from out of nowhere directly into my ear. "You ready for me to get you out of that thing, yet?"

I gulped down my water and tossed the cup in the trash. "I was ready before I ever put it on. The crowd's getting pretty sparse and probably feeling- good, anyway. I'm sure no one will notice us slip out. Plus, there's only about thirty minutes until the DJ calls it a night."

"Good," he said, wrapping me in his arms. "Mrs. Rowan Vera Miller. Let's go home and consummate our marriage." He nipped at my earlobe with his teeth. "Maybe practice putting another baby inside you."

Lyndsay Marie

ONE
Katie

"I'm pregnant."

"You're what?" I shot off the couch.

"You heard me. I said I'm pregnant! We're having a baby!" Rowan screeched into my ear.

"I know I heard you, but normal people say hey or hi when someone answers the phone."

"Since when have you known me to do anything normal?"

"Valid point. So holy shit, Rowan! You're pregnant? How did that happen?"

She laughed. "Un, I think we both know how it happened."

"You know what I mean. I think we both know *how*." It was a huge surprise—I know it had to be to them too. The last time Rowan had announced she was expecting a baby was at hers and Wes's wedding reception around this time last year. Unfortunately, not a month later, they had to call everyone they knew and tell them that she had unexpectedly lost the baby. She and Wes were devastated. Hell, I think we all were. It was the second time she'd been through that. I didn't think she wanted to try again.

My mom barged into the room, carrying a cardboard box in her arms. "Who's pregnant?" she blurted out.

I covered the phone mouthpiece. "Shh!"

Rowan laughed. "That must be your mom. Tell her I said hi."

I uncovered the phone. "Sorry, Rowe. She walked right in on that one."

"No worries," Rowan said. "It's okay if she knows."

Mom waved me off. "And I'm walking right back out. We'll catch up later. Tell Rowan congratulations." Then she disappeared from the room without so much as another word. Not knowing all the details of the latest gossip, even if it involved my life, would eat at her until she knew.

I put my attention back on my BFF. "Mom says congrats. Ah! I'm so happy for y'all."

"Thank you, thank you. Speaking of your mom, how's the big move going? Y'all getting everything settled?"

I dabbed away a tiny bead of sweat dripping down my temple with the edge of the sleeve of my T-shirt, careful not to wipe away my foundation. Someone could've at least picked a better month than June to force a family to uproot their lives.

"If by move you mean me living with my parents against my free will in my thirties? Then I'd say it's going swimmingly well. Everything is just fine and freaking dandy."

One of us laughed. Hint: it wasn't me.

"Aw, come on, Sugar. Don't sound so excited. Your parents are amazing people!"

"Indeed they are. Why don't you come live with them, then?"

"Oooh, no, I didn't say I wanted all of that."

"Hmm. Exactly." I gulped down water from my Las Vegas souvenir bottle. "But you're right. They are amazing…from across town. Not across the house."

"They just moved in. It can't be *that* bad."

"Yet," I said, as if to finish off her unspoken words. She held back a giggle. I was just glad someone found humor in all of this because I, for one, was not a fan of having my life unexpectedly turned upside down. Expecting the unexpected at work was one thing—that was part of the job—but having my consistent and organized life in complete disarray was another.

"Don't worry your pretty little head. It won't be for forever."

"Yeah, right. It doesn't feel like it." Even though she couldn't see me, that didn't stop me from sticking my tongue out at her. "That still doesn't mean I want to *live* with them…*again*." Unfortunately, that had been my—hopefully temporary—reality. There was a reason I'd moved out at seventeen, and it hadn't been because I'd been swept off my feet by Prince Charming on a white horse. It was because my mother drove me up a damned wall with all of her demands on me to give one hundred percent, one hundred and ten percent of the time.

Now here we were full circle damned near fifteen years later. Everything happened so fast. Less than four weeks ago, my parents received a certified letter, hand-delivered by a local law enforcement officer. The letter declared domain over all of their land and the house they'd purchased just a few years ago. They'd bought the acreage and farmhouse with the intent of one day turning it all into an actual farm with livestock and gardens. Mom's dreams went up in smoke, Dad lit up a smoke, and the entire process from appraisal to paycheck took one solid month—a whole thirty days. Hiring a lawyer to fight the process would have cost them everything they'd owned, regardless. To them it hadn't been worth the fight.

So, the three of us—Dad, Mom, and myself, with the help of a couple of neighbors—had spent the past few days moving most of their things out of their big house and into a storage unit. Their necessities came with them here.

"True, but hopefully time will fly by, and you'll be out on your own again soon enough, or they'll take that fat check they got and buy another farm somewhere else."

"Who knows. You know how damned picky my mother is. Look how long it took them to find that place."

She sighed. "True. Good luck, I guess."

"Thanks. So, you're gonna have a baby! This is exciting."

"Oh, it is. We're pretty ecstatic. Scared shitless too."

"I bet you are. It'll work out this time."

"We sure hope so."

"Well, give me all the details, I need to know everything."

"There's not much to tell. So far, not very many people know. We've had to keep this one under wraps for a while for obvious reasons."

"I don't blame y'all. Wait. What do you mean for a while? How far along are you?"

"Umm, well—"

"Spit it out, Rowan."

"Like five months?"

"Five months! Are you shitting me right now? You've been pregnant for five months?"

"Yes?"

"And you didn't freaking tell me?"

"I'm so sorry."

Five months? Insane! I could never keep a secret like that for that long.

"So, when are you due?"

"October."

Keep reading here book two —
https://www.amazon.com/dp/B095KR2NHG

thank you

www.AuthorLyndsayMarie.com

Visit me on Amazon —
https://www.amazon.com/author/lyndsaymarie